Mud Pie

a novel

R. L. Greene

DIVERGENT MIND LLC

La Veta, Colorado

Divergent Mind LLC
P.O. Box 1053
La Veta, CO 81055

ISBN 978-1-947803-04-6

Copyright © 2020 Roger L. Greene All rights reserved.

Greene, Roger L.

Mud Pie/R.L. Greene. First edition.

212 pages

Jacket content and design by R.L. Greene
Images Shutterstock License

Summary: A bored socialite's life is turned upside down when a landslide plants a family of hillbillies in the back yard of her exquisite estate. Fuedin' and potshots give way to an unlikely and heart-changing love.

[1. Comedy – Fiction.   2. Friendship – Fiction.   3. Loss – Fiction.

4. Forgiveness – Fiction. 5. Ideals – Fiction   6. Acceptance – Fiction.

7. Understanding – Fiction.]

CONTENTS

Chapter One

A Big ol' Slice of It

"It cannot hinder the view of the fountain. This is crucial. That is where the portrait will be taken." With a flail of her hand and her peach sundress floating behind her, Evelyn Chatsblythe, the not-so-young, yet strikingly beautiful mistress of the superlative Italian Renaissance estate begins a brisk stride across an expanse of emerald green lawn.

Following her toward the marble fountain nestled near the base of a rugged canyon wall is Kenneth, a well-dressed party planner, frantically tapping an i-Pad. "Portrait?" he asks while checking his notes. "I wasn't aware you needed a photographer."

Evelyn dismisses his concern with a wave of her hand. "Oh God no. I wouldn't allow you to handle something as important as that. I'm having Vincent fly in from Paris." Evelyn strokes the contours of her face. "Vince knows how to bring out my classic cheekbones." The mistress spins about to position herself elegantly on the rim of the fountain and crosses her long legs beneath the flowing fabric. "I will sit here and open my arms as if to say *welcome* to my guests. It is at that precise moment that the balloons will be released behind me and Vincent will capture the moment as only *he* can do." Evelyn spreads her arms, then looks up and feigns delight as she pretends to watch make-believe balloons soar heavenward.

As Kenneth watches Evelyn's imaginary balloons soar past the canyon's craggy, arid walls of succulents, juniper, cedar and sumac, he manages a lukewarm, "Oh."

"Oh?" Evelyn repeats scathingly as she abandons her elegant pose. She blinks her synthetic cobalt blues with a degree of pseudo-moral outrage that is typically only experienced by the 1%. "Do you not comprehend the paradox that conveys how I've maintained my child-like sense of wonder even as I enter my forty-third year with the kind of dignified grace that others appreciate so about me?"

After blinking a few times with the kind of stunned disbelief usually reserved for the remaining 99% of us, Kenneth's eyebrows rise ever-so-slightly. "Of course."

"So *now* do you understand why the tent cannot block the view of the fountain?"

Kenneth sighs with metered impatience. "Missus Chatsblythe, if you want a tent, you're going to have to sacrifice the perfect view of something. Could we place it near the garden, perhaps?"

"The garden?" Evelyn brings two fingers with impeccably manicured nails to her collagen-enhanced lips. "How can I have the perfect party if my guests cannot enjoy the splendor of the garden? The dignity of a formal garden cannot be compromised by a monstrous tent looming nearby. Do they not teach you anything at party school? It will make the grounds look as if the circus has come to town and a herd of elephants and a troupe of clowns are due to arrive at any moment."

She blinks.

Kenneth blinks.

"So, you want to forgo the tent?"

"Heavens no." Evelyn rises indignantly from the fountain rim. "Are you from this planet? How do you not know that Southern California is coming into its rainy season? And if it doesn't rain, the sun will almost certainly be too intense. And it could be migration season. Think of the disaster a flock of hugely shitting birds flying overhead could cause. We must have a tent..."

"Near the pool?" Kenneth quickly suggests.

Evelyn winces.

She is about to argue how the splendor of the dozen marble Greek nudes that surround the pool are certain to be compromised by a looming tent when a tin can bounces down the canyon wall and draws their attention. As they shield their eyes against the sun, the can springs from an outcropping, soars across the flawless blue sky, plunges earthward, then splashes into the fountain where it bobs happily in the churning water.

"Oh ick." Evelyn's lip curls.

While curiously looking up the hill, Kenneth distractedly proposes, "A few small canopies would probably suffice. Only a fraction of your guests have sent confirmations."

"What do you mean by *only a fraction*?"

"Out of two hundred invitations, only thirty-five have accepted."

"Did you address them correctly?" Evelyn demands with her eyes blazing. "Did you remember to mail them? Tell me, how have you managed such a catastrophe?"

"I have over one hundred regrets, madam."

With her jaw hanging limp, Evelyn stares at the party planner and blinks as she is prone to do in situations such as this.

"It might be a good idea to downsize the festivities," Kenneth cautiously suggests.

After two more blinks and a dozen beats of a heart only momentarily broken, Evelyn turns her attention to the can bobbing in the fountain. She pulls a small bell from her pocket and rings it desperately.

Floyd, an ancient gardener, hobbles around the pool house, then stops.

The bell ceases. Evelyn calls, "Another piece of crap has fallen into the fountain." She quivers. "Oh, and I found a weed growing over by the Eleanor Roosevelt. If you thought it was a flower, it is not. Flowers do not have leaves that go..." Evelyn twists her hands and arms grotesquely.

After standing motionless a moment, Floyd waves acknowledgment, shakes his head wearily, then with a bow-legged old man shuffle, disappears back behind the pool house.

"Where is that senile old man going? Does he think I rang for my health?" Frenetically ringing the bell, Evelyn pursues the weary gardener in a determined march. "Floyd. *Floyd.* I meant now, *not* five minutes from now."

With despair eating what is left of his soul, Kenneth lets his i-Pad fall limply to his side, shakes his head as Floyd had done, then trudges after Evelyn. "The tent, Missus Chatsblythe. Could I have a decision about the tent?"

Branches begin to rustle in the wooded cleft that runs up the canyon wall. Sausalito Jones, a wiry sixteen-year-old, makes his way down the hillside while wiping the juice of canned peaches from the corners of his mouth. Sporting hollow cheeks accented by smudges of filth, he stops and peers through the branches as Evelyn's brisk pursuit and shrill screeching, followed by Kenneth's silent plodding behind, both vanish around the far side of the pool house.

His grimy baseball cap partially obscures equally soiled, scraggly hair. With a squint of his dull brown eyes, he spits, plucks a stem of grass from the hillside, then places it in his mouth. Ratty overalls that hang loosely from his bare shoulders expose a good three inches of hairy ankles above equally distressed leather boots at their other end. With a bucket in one hand and a shovel in the other, he continues his descent with the kind of long, slow gait favored by the mountainfolk of times gone by.

There are certain disasters that befall mankind. Only rarely do they happen on a Tuesday morning. Occasionally they entail hysteria. Usually they involve the slightly aging mistress whose child-like wonder and dignified grace are the envy of all.

So it is that on this Tuesday morning, across town, in the engineering lab of a high-tech prototype developer, several professionals in lab coats are huddled together at a table. Unaware that disaster has occurred, Carter Chatsblythe, the impeccably dressed CEO of *Proto Precision* and long-suffering husband of the mistress of the estate, is studying schematics along with his crew of engineers.

The shapely legs of the firm's receptionist tug at her short skirt as she enters the area in an urgent stride. Her stiletto heels click briskly on the floor while a great deal of wailing emits from the cordless phone she carries at her side. She approaches the group with wide eyes and addresses Mr. Chatsblythe. "I'm so sorry to interrupt sir, but it's your wife." She extends the phone to Carter. All freeze as a particularly piercing wail comes from the receiver.

Carter looks at the phone with apprehension, then mouths the words, "I'm not here." He gestures her away just as a bout of sobbing begins to seep from the phone. After taking in the disillusioned expressions of the engineers – for what kind of jerk would do such a thing to his wife in her moment of despair – Carter flares his nostrils, sighs with exasperation, then extends his hand for the phone.

He holds the receiver to his ear and laboriously begins, "Evelyn. - Evelyn. - Evelyn, - honey, - dear, - could you calm down? Evelyn. - Evelyn." He looks at the faces of the engineers and smiles pathetically. "Evelyn. Evelyn, I need you to calm down."

The sobbing stops. Just as Carter opens his mouth to speak, a barrage of desperately high-pitched complaint spews from the receiver. While struggling to understand and only marginally able to keep the phone anywhere near his ear, Carter comments as the rare opportunity presents itself. "My God - Floyd did what? - To whom? - *Murdered?*" The engineers gasp and the receptionist draws her hands up to her mouth.

Their expressions of stunned disbelief are like those that usually occur when first hearing of disaster on an otherwise pleasant and ordinary Tuesday morning.

If anyone should ever want to know, it takes a Ferrari 308 nineteen minutes and forty-two seconds to speed from Proto Precision to 1219 Happy Canon Drive. Carter Chatsblythe now stands on the expanse of emerald-green lawn at Evelyn's side. Both look down at exposed soil of a shovel-sized hole where a few rose petals are all that remain of Evelyn's prized Eleanor Roosevelt rosebush.

Happily, the weed growing next to it is quite undisturbed.

Evelyn's face is streaked with rivulets of black mascara wetted by tears that glisten in the midday sun. Beneath a very ordinary hazel eye, one of her cobalt blue contact lenses is stuck to her cheek. She sniffles into a tissue, rivets her eyes on the gardener, then speaks bitterly. "It was that bastard, Floyd."

Carter looks from the hole, over to the edge of the garden where Floyd stands in the shade of a cluster of Palm trees with his hands clasped before him. His head is bowed solemnly – in reverence for the deceased – one would imagine.

"Evelyn, honey, Floyd doesn't strike me as the type."

"Oh, he's cunning. Don't let that feeble old man act fool you. He's a maniac. Make him tell you where he hid her."

After a heavy sigh, Carter trudges away.

With crossed arms and a tapping foot, Evelyn seethes with vehemence as she watches Carter approach Floyd.

"How's it going, Floyd?" Carter asks wearily.

Floyd's gaunt eyes rise up to face Carter. A slow smack of Floyd's chops that are comprised of scraggly whiskers and toothless gums, precede his response. "Not bad. The crazy bitch is driving me nuts though."

"I hear ya," Carter commiserates because right now the vivacious, exciting woman he married twenty years ago has indeed become a crazy bitch that is also slowly driving him nuts. "Listen," he asks bluntly, "did you kill the damn rosebush?"

"Wish I'd thought of it." Floyd pulls his whiskered chin up to his nose.

Carter studies the sincerity in the dreary eyes of the master gardener who looks like a bum but knows his stuff and so far has not been run off by the mistress of the estate who happens to be very good at running off the help. "Hmmm. Well, carry on then." Carter starts to turn away, then turns back. "And try not to act old. It's making her suspicious."

With a cursory nod that is followed by more heartfelt shaking of his head, Floyd ambles away. Carter glances to

7

where Kenneth, worn, has collapsed against one of the classical Greek nude statues that surround the pool. The party planner mouths the words, "Help me," before allowing his eyes to roll back into his head.

Until the mistress's forty-third birthday has passed, *help me* will be the plea of all mortals in the realm of the semi-notorious Evelyn Chatsblythe. For you see, the mistress of the grand villa is completely oblivious to the touch of irony her personality brings to the winding road known as Happy Canyon Drive that runs a mile deep into a rugged canyon of absolutely preposterous wealth.

With night having fallen, Evelyn, wearing a flowing nightgown, stands at the master suite bay window with her arms folded. Carter, in plaid pajamas, sits on their bed looking at Evelyn's slender back. With weariness, "I'm sure everything is going to be perfect. Size doesn't matter. Could we please focus on the thirty-five that are coming and not the one-hundred-sixty something who have other plans?"

"Everyone knows when my birthday is. Why would they make other plans?"

"I'm sure it was an oversight."

"One hundred and sixty something oversights?"

"Shit happens."

"They don't like me."

"I'm sure they adore you. You are the epitome of good taste and high society. Even with a smallish turnout, I'm sure you will have the most fabulous birthday since Cleopatra."

"You're placating me. I hate it when you placate me."

"Whatever darling. I'm tired and I'm going to sleep. Good night." Carter turns out the light on his nightstand, gets under the covers and turns away on his side.

It is silent in the room now bathed in subtle light.

"Why can't I fire the help?"

The motionless lump beneath the covers sighs. Carter explains in a slightly muffled and somewhat annoyed, mechanical tone, "Because there aren't enough people in the county – and possibly the state – for you to fire everyone that annoys you. So, unfortunately for you, they are my employees, not yours, therefore you cannot."

"Are you my husband or my father? I am not a child."

The lump is unresponsive.

"Then I will be sleeping in my retreat." Evelyn huffs as she glares at the bed and its man-shaped satin comforter. She storms out of the room and slams the door behind her.

A groan emits from under the comforter.

The recently slammed door opens.

After flicking on a myriad of light switches to illuminate the room to roughly the brightness of the face of the sun, Evelyn marches in. She grabs the remote, turns on both the television and stereo, cranks them to an unbearable volume, then drops the remote into a vase of freshly cut orchids. "Humph." She sneers at the covers, exits and re-slams the door.

With her gown flapping wildly behind her, Evelyn marches angrily from the master suite, along the curved balcony that overlooks the superlative living room below. She comes to a door near the top of the staircase, opens it, careens inside and – because doors are basically perfect for slamming – slams it shut behind her.

Her retreat is illuminated by a shaft of moonlight entering the windows. Evelyn forgoes the lights, then with an arm stretched before her and the other trailing behind like the overly dramatic actresses of 40's and 50's black-and-white overly dramatic movie era, she glides directly toward an ornate canopied feather bed in the middle of the room, lands face-first on the bed and sinks into its softness.

She is still.

She is also unable to breathe.

There is a rustling of satin as Evelyn thrashes about to curl onto her side.

Lines of distress are etched around her perfect features. Her hazel eyes dart anxiously side to side. After lying there a moment, she sits and twists around with another rustling of fabric, then flops back against a mound of lace pillows. She lays still only a moment, then reaches around so that she can take a porcelain doll from the nightstand. She clutches it to her bosom, rests her cheek on the top of its head and hugs it tenderly.

"I'm not perfect anymore," she whispers to the doll. She draws and expels a forlorn breath, then holds the doll into the shaft of moonlight. "You will always be perfect. You will always be young. Everyone will always want you." Evelyn gazes into the doll's senseless vibrant blue irises.

The creases of Evelyn's distress begin to fade from her face. Finally, she smiles a tiny little smile and lifts a finger to move a lock of synthetic doll hair back from a hand-painted face. "Always perfect," she repeats, sniffs, then bites her lip. She gazes at the doll's flawless appearance and smiles tenderly.

Outside the villa's walls, clouds roll beneath the lunar brilliance, then churn against the moon's bright face until it and its light are extinguished. Far beyond the canyon wall, the sky flashes and distant thunder rolls.

The next morning finds Evelyn holding a robe tightly around her waist as torrents of rain douse the glass panes of the French doors that encircle the breakfast nook. While sipping from a steaming mug of coffee, she watches the storm with concern, then furtively turns toward the telephone.

The raspy voice of the cook and housekeeper, Mrs. Gilbert booms. "Don't even think about it, missy."

"I wasn't, I..." Evelyn turns to find the intense eyes of Mrs. Gilbert staring her down from across the kitchen. In the weathered full face of the earthy woman, there is a knowledge that crumbles Evelyn's innocent ruse. "What if the ground gets soggy?"

"Then ya wear boots. Ain't nothin' your mister is gonna be able to do about the rain."

The two stare at one another.

If one was to imagine the hearty stock of woman prevalent in pioneer lore from the years 1650 through 1850 that could till ten acres by hand, milk cows, slaughter chickens, birth one dozen children, and chop firewood; Mrs. Gilbert would come to mind. Like Floyd, she knows her stuff and is impervious to the slings and arrows of Mrs. Chatsblythe.

Surmising the stand-off will not go her way, Evelyn tosses her hair back, then begins to stride from the room. "Then I'm going shopping. Have Bernard bring the car around." She hesitates in the arched doorway with her back toward the housekeeper.

"In an hour.

"Or two.

"First, I will be bathing." With another arrogant shake of her head, Evelyn proceeds toward one, or depending on her mood, possibly two of the mansion's ten bathrooms, for it is her prerogative to mess them all up if she so pleases – and she frequently does. After watching her only momentarily, Mrs. Gilbert shakes her head, rolls her eyes, then wipes the counter with her dishcloth.

Up the canyon wall, beyond its crest, in an arid woods of low, twisted trees, succulents and cacti, stands the faded remains of a circa 1950's pink house trailer with an improvised corrugated steel shed roof built atop it. Water streams from the tin panels onto the saturated mud that surrounds the humble abode. A quarter-acre of rusted junk, chicken coops and goat pens encircle the homestead to complete the ambiance.

While rain pelts the metal roof with a constant din, Sausalito Jones sits at a tiny table, sucking on his lip as he concentrates to write on a piece of paper before him. His mother, Loretta, a gaunt woman of sickly pallor with dark rings beneath her eyes, lays propped up in bed peering as best she can at his work.

Not totally unlike a cheery bouquet of fresh-cut flowers and shiny helium orbs bearing well wishes of better health, the Eleanor Roosevelt rosebush sits unceremoniously in a bucket at her bedside. Her labored voice is weak as Loretta advises, "Watch yer penmanship, Sausalito. I kin't hardly make that out."

"Okay, Mama," Sausalito drawls, then redoubles his effort. The relative quiet is broken when the door opens. Cincinnati, an innocent boy of eleven with long hair and ratty clothes steps inside, soaked to the bone. He quickly shuts the door, then after a wary glance at his mother and brother, wiggles his shoulders out of his saturated coat.

"Find anything interestin', young'un?" Loretta asks with a wheeze.

"Dead bird was all."

Sausalito looks up from his studies with hopeful eyes. "Eatin' bird?"

"Jus' a poor baby felled out'a the nes' and drown'd.

12

Weren't no bigger than yer thumb." The boy holds up his thumb.

Sausalito exhales with disappointment. Loretta nods, then launches into a coughing fit of wheezes and deep rattles. Her sons watch impassively as the fit passes. While drying himself with a towel, Cincinnati interjects, "You ain't soundin' so good, Mama."

"I'm okay, honey-pot. The molds stirred up from the rain make it hard to breathe. You jus' worry about yer studies and that will be comfort 'nough for me."

Sausalito sternly pushes a book across the small table. Cincinnati looks at it, then defiantly walks over to Loretta's bedside. While looking deep into her ailing eyes, he strokes her hair affectionately. She runs her hand over his wet hair with a grateful smile. The boy leans close, kisses her, then walks back to the table, sits, pulls the book close and takes a pencil in hand. Loretta watches only momentarily, then lets her head fall back into her pillow.

"Sausalito," she speaks with pure exhaustion, "you got all them papers we talked about?"

"Yes, Mama. They's all safe and secure."

"That's my boy." She breathes arduously. "And you know who to talk to at the bank?"

"Missus Conley. I got it Mama."

"You're a good son. Both a' you are. I'm very proud to have been your mother."

"Thank you, Mama."

The boys look at one another with a full understanding of the words, "proud to have been."

On a street lined with exclusive boutiques, a black limousine slowly drives through the pouring rain. Bernard, the placid middle-aged chauffer at the wheel, looks straight ahead with vacant detachment. Behind him, in a state of

13

near desperation, Evelyn cranes her neck as she tries to look out all the windows at once. "Toni's...no. Holland Brothers... um, no. Maybe something to eat. Oh gosh, no. I can't gain any weight before the party. Maybe a cappuccino? No, no, that makes me hyper."

From her perch on the edge of her seat, Evelyn suddenly points. "Pomades! Pull over. I need a fragrance. That is what I need. Bernard, what are you doing? I said, *pull over.*"

"I'm looking for a parking place, madam."

"Ugh. Would you look? It's at least three stores down now. You just passed a loading zone. Are you watching what you're doing at all? Over there! Over there! Park in the bus stop."

Bernard's lip tugs ever so slightly as he tightens his grip and yanks the wheel. Dislodged from her precarious position, Evelyn shrieks as her feet fly up and she tumbles to the floorboard. The limousine jerks to a halt with another happy thump or two from the back.

Bernard smiles with devious, yet placid delight.

Moments later, a not-as-amused-and-now-really-soggy Bernard rushes alongside Evelyn holding an umbrella to protect her from the rain. She strides along, pulling at her clothing. "I'm rumpled. How on earth did you get a position driving a car? That half-wit, Floyd, who is blind as a bat, could have maneuvered better. You better believe Mister Chatsblythe will hear about this."

A tow truck cruises past them, unnoticed. As it nears the limousine parked in the bus stop with its hazard flashers on, the truck slows and its yellow lights begin to flash.

Inside Pomades, a drenched Bernard opens the door for Evelyn, who enters regally. He collapses the umbrella, steps in behind her, then stands just inside the entrance. She spins around and looks at him dryly – which is somewhat ironic if you think about it. "What are you doing?"

He looks at her blankly.

"I don't like to be watched."

Looking then between Evelyn and the approaching salespeople and considering his options, Bernard quietly steps back outside, opens the umbrella, and stands in the rain.

The salespeople are then forced to retreat as Evelyn parades along the counter without so much as stopping to smell the fragrances. "Junk. Sludge. Rot. Urine."

Iron gates open for two taxis to pull into the estate. Both stop in the still pouring rain near the mansion's front door. Evelyn gets out of one, and Bernard, the other. She pops open the sole umbrella, then proceeds into the house in a huff. Bernard simply walks to the front steps in a slouch, sits in the torrent of rain and buries his face in his hands as the taxies depart. Floyd happens to be ambling about the grounds in a yellow slicker collecting worms. Worms, if you didn't know, make lumps in the grass – and lumps are not acceptable to Mrs. Chatsblythe. Anyway, Floyd approaches Bernard and observes him through the water pouring off his visor. "Handicap space?" he ventures, then pulls his chin up to his nose.

"Bus stop."

"Crazy bitch," Floyd mutters, slowly shakes his head, then hobbles away with his writhing can of worms.

With evening having fallen, the rain continues but has mercifully reduced to a steady drizzle. Evelyn sits on her bed with her knees drawn up to her chest, eyes downcast

15

and her lower lip protruding in a pout. With his hands firmly on his hips, Carter speaks through the frown that cannot find its way off his face. "You have to be nice to people. You have to be patient..."

"Even when they're imbeciles?" Evelyn's color-of-the-day fluorescent green eyes dart up at him with a nasty glare.

"Just because they don't do what you want, precisely when you want, does not make them imbeciles."

"They are here to serve me. They're serve-ants."

Carter sighs. "They are here to help us run this home. We can move into a three-bedroom rancher with lap siding and neighbors ten feet away where you can cook, clean, garden, wear slippers in the supermarket, and drive yourself around town in a station wagon if you'd like."

Evelyn's face contorts horribly. Her mouth falls open.

While pointing sternly, Carter continues. "That's about where I'm at. One more hysterical phone call. One more towing charge. One more impound. One more..."

Evelyn's eyes narrow hatefully.

Carter returns his hand to his hip. "From now on you will let Bernard drive the car, Floyd take care of the grounds and Missus Gilbert run the house **without** your directives and demands. I trust them. I pay them to do what they do. And in my opinion, they do it well."

"And if I'm miserable, that means nothing to you?"

"It's either you or the rest of the world." Carter holds his hands like a scale that is suddenly put off-balance and shrugs.

Evelyn's perfectly plump upper lip curls hatefully.

Up the hill in the dismal pink trailer, a kerosene lamp burns brightly. Loretta coughs and gags as Sausalito cradles her in his arms. Cincinnati holds a steaming tin cup under her nose. Sausalito cajoles, "Breathe the steam, Mama. It'll break up the congestion."

"It's tea, Mama. Take a sip," Cincinnati pleads.

Loretta gently pushes it aside and turns away, coughing too hard to speak. The boys look at one another, then Sausalito lays his mother back into the pillows, rises abruptly, and walks to the door.

The shaft of light from the opening door illuminates a dozen pairs of yellow eyes that instantly appear in the blackness of the woods. Sausalito steps out into the drizzling rain and softly closes the door behind him. Once again in darkness, the reflecting yellow eyes disappear into the black. Within a couple steps, Sausalito's posture crumbles. When he begins to sob, the piercing yips and wails of a dozen coyotes accompany his weeping.

The next morning finds birds singing in bright sunshine. Only a few wisps of fog linger along the canyon walls. Inside the mansion, Mrs. Gilbert is busily preparing breakfast when Evelyn bounces into the kitchen wearing very stylish sweats accessorized with fuzzy ankle warmers. With astoundingly good cheer and brandishing tiny pink plastic dumbbells, she dances to an imaginary rhythm. "Good morning, Missus Gilbert. It has stopped raining."

Mrs. Gilbert eyes the cheerful mood and tie-dyed contacts that adorn the mistress's eyes. "Good morning, Evelyn. You are one lucky lady. The forecast says it will be nice for your big day." Mrs. Gilbert adds a garnish to the gourmet breakfast she has prepared, then places the china plate on the table with a proud chef's, "Voila."

Evelyn stops dancing.

"Oh," she says with profound disappointment while looking at the plate with sour dismay. "I didn't want that today."

The two look at one another. After unceremoniously

pulling out the chair adjacent to the plate, Mrs. Gilbert cocks her head toward it ever so slightly. The crazed look in her eyes and flared nostrils imply a threat. After gauging the situation and weight classification of the contestants, Evelyn sheepishly makes her way over to the chair, but stops short of sitting. "Maybe Bernard would like that and I could just have a yogurt." She smiles ingratiatingly.

"Listen lady, you will eat this or I will stuff it in your ears."

Sausalito and Cincinnati sit at the table looking at their hands while Loretta fades. Her breathing is irregular and the rattle, louder. "Mama's dying, huh?" Cincinnati asks.

Sausalito nods. "Not much longer now."

"Couldn't we git her to a hospital?"

"You know she don't want no part of no hospital. This is where she wants to be and we's who she wants to be with."

"I'm a little scared. I don't want Mama to die."

Sausalito can only look at his brother because both of them already know her wishes well.

Suddenly, a groan crawls the length of the trailer and the boys find themselves jostled a bit. They make odd faces at one another as another groan begins beneath them. "What the heck?" Sausalito's wondering is cut short by a sudden lurch. The trailer and the earth beneath it begin to move. The boys reach for something solid to hold on to as speed begins to pick up. Suddenly, everything tilts. With dishes and books crashing around them, they holler in fright.

Meanwhile, in the breakfast nook, round one of the Happy Canyon title match is underway. Evelyn bobs and weaves from one side of the table and throws not-very-threatening punches in the air with her tiny weights. Growling lowly from the other side, Mrs. Gilbert holds the breakfast plate like it's a cream-pie about to be thrown.

The chandelier above them begins to rattle.

Both freeze. Their eyes slowly roll upward to the shimmering crystals. "Earthquake," they shout, then bolt for the French doors.

They exit the house in a sprint just as a swath of earth slides down a cleft in the canyon wall, then plows across the emerald lawn. Trees and bushes still intact, the sliver of land rushes alongside the mansion. In a matter of seconds, it slogs to a halt like a train having rolled into a station. The pink trailer atop the mound now sits nearly even with the second floor of the mansion. The lower jaws of both women hang limp. The plate and its gourmet breakfast falls from Mrs. Gilbert's hand onto the patio with a crash.

Inside the trailer, the boys look at each other with wide eyes. It is absolutely silent. They rise, then step over a litter of dishes to get to the door. They step outside, then cross the muddy yard as frightened goats, freed from their pens and chickens, loose from their coops, dart and flap about around them. The boys thrash through the bushes, come to the edge, and look down on the manicured grounds of the estate spread out below.

Mrs. Gilbert and Evelyn peer back up at the boys from beneath hands they have brought up to shield their eyes from the sun. The boys blink a few times, then look at one another. "Mama," they both shout, then slip and splash through the mud to rush back inside.

Loretta's mattress has slid onto the floor where she has sunk into her covers and pillows. Upon peeling them away, her boys find her eyes closed in peace. No breath comes from her slightly parted lips.

Cincinnati weeps into Sausalito's arms as they sit together on Loretta's mattress. Sausalito's voice cracks. "We's on our own now, little brother." He sniffs between sobs. "Mama done gone to heaven. She's lookin' down on us now, you can be assured."

He cranes his neck to look out the dingy window toward the mansion of the glistening estate they landed in. "Her spirit done some mysterious and powerful work 'fore it left her. Lord have mercy on what befalls us now."

Evelyn and Mrs. Gilbert gaze up the canyon wall where the long gash of newly exposed earth extends beyond the rim. Just then, a tin can rolls from the mound in front of them, bounces off the exposed tangle of roots that protrude from the muddy slide, then lands on the grass. The two women stare at it, share an incredulous look, then creep toward the mound. They tiptoe across the soggy lawn, around the corner of the mansion to see where the landslide has stopped only inches from the iron front fence.

At the leading edge of the slog, Floyd's two black rubber boots protrude from the muck.

Chapter Two

Not the Damn Roses

"Ahhhhh," Mrs. Gilbert screams, hikes up her apron and skirt, then runs splashing like an out-of-control locomotive across the grass toward Floyd's protruding boots.

Evelyn stands where she is.

Mrs. Gilbert barrels up, then slides to a stop at Floyd's feet like she's coming into third. She clamors into the bog and frantically begins to dig. At a point, she turns toward Evelyn and calls with desperation. "Evelyn, help!"

While the housekeeper resumes digging, Evelyn looks at her perfectly polished nails, then at the ooze now seeping around her sparkly pink shoes. *"Ummmm."*

She runs back toward the house.

The front of the slog is a frantic scene of flying mud, housekeeper butt and housekeeper elbows until Floyd's head pops up. A toothless gasp follows. Bernard, wearing his housecoat and obviously just awakened, appears from nowhere, spots the emergency, dashes over and jumps into the mud at Mrs. Gilbert's side.

As Bernard takes over, the housekeeper rolls over and collapses in the slime. In a few moments, Floyd wriggles one arm free and then another. He scoops mud from his eyes and spits it from his mouth. When Mrs. Gilbert catches her breath, she resumes digging alongside Bernard. Exhausted, she and Bernard finally take hold of Floyd and

21

pull him to his feet.

Just then, Evelyn runs up to them wearing mink trimmed boots and holding a small hand trowel at the ready in her elbow-length, white-gloved hand.

Help has arrived.

Thank the Lord.

The brothers go from place-to-place walking about the top of the landslide with shovels in hand, occasionally stopping, then looking all directions. "How about over there?" Cincinnati points out a clear area. The brothers walk over and survey the view, which happily overlooks the fountain.

After stomping around a bit, Sausalito nods. "Seems firm enough." He adds judiciously, "I think Mama would like it. She always did think fountains was somethin' special." He plunges a shovel into the soggy earth. "You picked a good spot, young'un."

Cincinnati smiles crookedly. "Ought'a be easy diggin'." He grunts as he plunges his shovel in alongside his brother's.

Evelyn stands at the French doors of the master suite balcony holding bejeweled opera binoculars to her eyes with a wand, observing the two boys as they dig deeper and deeper. The growling of her stomach that enjoyed no breakfast, and so far no lunch, prompts her to look at the clock which presently reads 12:35 p.m.

She approaches an intercom panel on the wall, then hesitantly raises a finger to push the button.

She withdraws it.

She raises it.

She withdraws it.

Her stomach growls. She walks a few steps to the

master suite door, opens it, and peers cautiously down the wide hall. After summoning her courage, she throws her head back, steps out into the hall, then boldly strides past successive portraits of birthdays 30-42. The shadows of her classic cheekbones and diminishing smiles of child-like wonder are professionally captured against identical backdrops of colorful balloons soaring heavenward.

Floyd, Bernard and Mrs. Gilbert all sit together over a huge muddy puddle that oozes out from beneath the table in the breakfast nook. Muddy footprints track all over the kitchen. Still shivering, the staff is donned in an ungodly assortment of towels, blankets and coats. The hair that isn't matted down to their scalps, stands straight up in twisted clumps. The dishes from their completed lunch litter the table. The scent of mutiny is in the air as Mrs. Gilbert caresses a bottle of strong whiskey in her rough hands. None of the bunch appears to be overly pleased.

Evelyn keeps her head held high as she sails into the kitchen with her eyes purposely averted from the glares of her staff. After looking at the filthy floor and with a humph of disdain, she scans the likely places her lunch might be waiting for her. Seeing, and frankly expecting nothing, she proceeds to the refrigerator where she begins to rummage about. The vengeful glares of the staff follow Evelyn as she cobbles together an assortment of foods and condiments. After opening and closing cupboard after cupboard, she eventually finds a plate and a glass.

The staff continues to pass the bottle amongst themselves, taking swigs and looking more menacing with every guzzle. Evelyn glances their direction frequently, with her nose high and being careful not to make any sort of eye-contact. Her lunch finally prepared, she picks it up, leaves the entire mess on the counter, then is about to leave the room when she stops. While looking straightforward at no one, she speaks arrogantly. "I don't suppose any of you have bothered to call Mister Chatsblythe."

Silence.

"I don't know why you're mad at me, I was coming to help."

Silence.

"Ughhh. Servants." Evelyn huffs in disgust and leaves.

Evelyn is once again standing at her balcony doors watching through opera glasses as Cincinnati and Sausalito continue to shovel dirt from the hole that is now waist deep. The phone rings. She pulls it from her pocket, glances at it with annoyance, then answers. "Kenneth. How nice of you to *finally* return my call. Did I not specify on my several messages that this was an emergency? - Yes, I thought I had. - I would imagine that an emergency would solicit a more timely response but I suppose ignoring me has become a national pastime in the service industry. - Whatever. - Listen, there has been a catastrophe of Biblical proportions..."

It is mid-afternoon as Kenneth stands at Evelyn's side on the grounds of the estate looking up at the mound of earth. He looks up and down the entire length of the slog. "I thought you were exaggerating," he finally admits.

Evelyn rolls her eyes. "I rather doubt we can have it trucked away before Sunday and even if we could, the lawn would be a disaster, so I'm thinking we – and by we – I mean you – could cover it up with something."

Kenneth regards her oddly. "Cover it up? The landslide? With what?"

"A tent? I don't know. Isn't that your specialty?"

"Ma'am, this is the size of Rhode Island. I plan parties. This is – a natural disaster – an act-of-God – a freaking landslide. I can't cover this up."

"What about sheets? I've seen articles where entire canyons are covered with sheets – like miles and miles of them. Why can't you do that? I think the man's name is Cristo. Why don't you give him a call?"

Kenneth looks at her, speechless, then summons pure resolve. "Those things take years of planning and engineering and copious materials."

"What was I thinking?" Evelyn's eyes roll to new heights of contempt. "Well, if it's not too much to ask, maybe you could do something about that horrible shack on top of it. Send in a helicopter, hook up a cable and fly it away to a landfill or something."

"Missus Chatsblythe, I plan parties. I coordinate caterers and entertainers. I rent tables and chairs and tents and order cakes and acquire flowers and balloons."

Now it is Evelyn that is speechless – at least temporarily. She contributes only blinks of disbelief to the conversation. "So, you're saying you cannot even manage the disposal of a shack?"

"Amazingly, I don't clear landslides of structures with helicopters."

Evelyn's brow rises. "Could you put a tent over the ghastly thing then?"

"Yes, I probably could put a tent over it."

Evelyn raises a second eyebrow. "Probably?"

"It's someone's home. I'd have to get their permission."

"It's on my estate. That makes it my property. If it can't be flown away, it needs to be covered over. We have covenants, you know." She looks at it through her tiny binoculars and curls her lip. "And soon. Ugh. There are two semi-naked miniature cavemen wandering about up there with shovels digging a septic or something. You can go speak to them."

Kenneth releases a long breath, then steps away and walks along the mound looking at the tangle of roots that kept it together during the slide. He eventually takes hold of a root, glances down at his ruined patent leather shoes that are already ankle-deep in mire, pulls it up, and places it on a firm-looking root. Just as he starts to put his weight on the root, the cocking of a rifle draws his attention.

Sausalito stands above him humorlessly looking down a barrel that is pointed at a spot somewhere between Kenneth's eyes. Kenneth freezes. Twenty feet to his side, the cock of another rifle sounds. Cincinnati sights down another barrel aimed at his right ventricle.

"This here's private property," Sausalito advises.

"No trespassin'," Cincinnati confirms.

After stepping back down, Kenneth releases his grip on the root. He glances toward Evelyn, who watches with fearful eyes and an open mouth. Kenneth looks back at the boys and puts on his broad party planner smile. "Gentlemen, I was just coming to pay you a visit."

"No you ain't." Sausalito's barrel follows Kenneth's every motion.

The party planner's ingratiating smile remains. He gestures toward Evelyn. "We were concerned. Are you folks all right?"

"State yer business."

"Well, uh, neighbor, I was wondering if I might be able to do something to help you out. Any..."

"We're doin' fine."

"What I'd like to offer is..."

"I said, I reckon we're doin' fine."

Kenneth's smile fades. His hands come up in

surrender as he begins to back away. "Very well then. You all have a nice day." The guns remain on him as he retreats back to where Evelyn stands. When he takes a place beside her, the boy's barrels are raised skyward. With a nod of Sausalito's head, Cincinnati disappears back into the brush. Big brother disappears a moment later.

Kenneth looks at Evelyn with pursed lips. She blinks. He speaks. "Don't think that tent is going to happen." He adds in his best hillbilly-ese, "Don't reckon yer new neighbors are gonna cotton much to yer shindig, neither." Kenneth then adds in his regular voice and with all seriousness, "Until your problem with armed neighbors pointing guns at people is taken care of, I will not be jeopardizing anyone or anything here. I'm sorry, but as far as my services go, your event is officially postponed."

Crestfallen, Evelyn opens her mouth to speak, but is cut short by a now suddenly assertive party planner. "No, you know what, Missus Chatsblythe? It's cancelled – period. My business will survive without you as a client. Dealing with you has been… well… dreadfully unpleasant, to say the least. And this… I don't even know where to start. I will gladly refund your deposit less the expenses and deposits I've already incurred. Have a nice day."

As Carter Chatsblythe's red Ferrari creeps up the canyon boulevard that is now lined with looky-loos, news and emergency vehicles, he cranes his neck. "What the heck?" he asks himself. Finding the greatest concentration of activity outside the iron fence that surrounds his mansion, he sighs with weariness. "Oh Evelyn, what did you do now?"

He presses the remote that activates his gates. As they open, he proceeds onto the driveway. Just now able to see the giant landslide that protrudes beyond his home all the way to the front fence, he stops his car, opens his door and stands as the gates close behind him. "Huh," he comments, then looks at the canyon wall that is now missing its wooded cleft. "How did she manage that?"

A clamor of shouts from reporters and emergency workers clinging to the iron pickets are nearly lost in the deafening din of a helicopter that suddenly arrives and hovers above. Carter glances their way only momentarily and holds up a finger that he'll be just a moment, or possibly two.

Carter then walks across the front lawn to peer around the house. Finding the length of the slog extends all the way to the back of the estate, he considers the muck oozing around his shoes, then makes his way down the corridor between the mansion and the mound of earth.

Upon rounding the back of the house, he finds Evelyn seated by the pool leisurely lounging in the setting sun. She's already about three sheets to the wind when she raises a wine cooler his direction as if to toast him, kills it, then carelessly flings the bottle into the pool. It floats a short while, then sinks. She takes another bottle from a bowl of ice at her side and twists the cap off.

Looking again at the tangle of roots and earth, Carter peers all the way up and down the length of the slide. When he looks back at his wife, he finds another toast raised his way. Over on the mansion's veranda, his staff – now crusty with dried earth and in various stages of undress in the warm sun, are sprawled about in a drunken stupor. The bath towels and clothing that is draped over the patio furniture, along with trash now scattered about, brings to mind a hobo campsite. Yet to utter a word, Carter pulls his slack jaw shut then rapidly shakes his head as if to force himself out of a preposterously bad dream.

With the last rays of sunlight filtering over the canyon wall, long shadows have overtaken the estate. Carter sits at the kitchen table across from Evelyn who now holds an icepack to her head between copious guzzles of water. The telephone answering machine beside them blinks thirty-eight unheard messages. "I just can't believe you didn't call me," he complains. "Or at the very least pick up the damn phone for the authorities. It took me forty-five minutes to convince them we were all right and get them to leave. Lord knows who else tried to reach us."

Evelyn sets down her water, looks at her husband blankly, then raises her middle finger.

"Seriously?" he asks.

"Yeah. Serothly," Evelyn slurs. "Ath I recahl, you ordered me no' to cahl you. And ih's your precious s'aff thah didn't anshwer the goh-damh 'hone."

"But this really was an emergency…"

"Well, how shou' I know? I'm jus' a hysterical bi'ch mos' the time."

"Evelyn…"

"Anyhay, the par'y's cancelled. Thaht should mahe you haphy. Your s'aff's on strike and your pain-in-the-hass wife is going to bed." Evelyn pats his hand, stands unsteadily, then staggers toward the doorway. "Oh, yeah," she adds, "there are two hillbihlies livhing in the bah yard."

"Two what?" Carter leans forward.

"Hillbihlies," Evelyn emphatically repeats. "Wi' guns." She mimics holding a rifle and popping off a round in Carter's general direction.

"Hillbillies with guns?" he clarifies.

"Yoh betcha." Evelyn points and winks.

"In that shack? You mean to tell me that people are living in that shack?"

"Noh pehple," Evelyn slurs. *"Hillbihlies."*

Carter's face crunches incredulously.

Figure it ou', mister big-sho'." Evelyn raises the middle finger again, bows deeply, then departs. She yells from beyond the wall she has disappeared behind. "I'll be slee'ing in my reheat."

Standing at the balcony doors of the dimly lit master suit, Carter observes the neighborhood's newest inhabitants through camouflaged field binoculars. An evening campfire blazes in front of the pink trailer where Sausalito and Cincinnati are busily preparing and lighting torches. They rise, then begin walking and placing them along the top of the slog. "Freaking hillbillies." Carter nurses a Scotch, then resumes his surveillance. "How can there be hillbillies living in Happy Canyon? We're not zoned for hillbillies." He watches the boys return along the now-lighted trail to their homestead. They disappear into the trailer. After a bit, Sausalito reappears in the narrow doorway, obviously struggling to carry something through the opening.

After setting his Scotch down, Carter fine-tunes the glasses. They bring into focus a homemade stretcher now halfway out the door. It bears a human-shaped form wrapped in sheets. "Oh. My. God."

Finally, as Sausalito backs onto the steps, Cincinnati emerges from the doorway with the other end of the stretcher. The form on the board is at this point, unmistakably human. The two young men proceed to carry the body down the rickety steps.

Carter kills the lights altogether and opens the doors so that he can step out on the balcony unnoticed. "Oh. My. God," he repeats in a whisper.

The boys struggle to carry the stretcher through the yard of rusted junk. Their procession continues along the torch-lit pathway toward the grave they had dug. "I do not freaking believe this," Carter murmurs entirely to himself.

When Loretta's form is placed beside the hole, her sons kneel at her side. As the boys sob, a semi circle of yellow eyes watch from the surrounding foliage. After a while, the boys sling the handles of the stretcher in ropes and lower the form into the ground. "Oh. Dear. God."

Handfuls of dirt are tossed into the grave. A few words are said, then the boys begin to shovel earth into the hole.

Carter steps back into the house and quietly closes the doors. He sets the field glasses on a nearby table, downs his Scotch, rubs his eyes, then plops down in an overstuffed chair. His eyes shift side-to-side in the dark as he considers what he has witnessed.

As the grey predawn creeps across the sky, Carter, still in the chair, slumbers. At the muffled crowing of a rooster, his eyelids begin to flutter. His heavy lids open, then close. He shifts about, trying to find a comfortable position. Another cock-a-doodle-doo pulls him from his sleep. As his mind sharpens, he squints, then looks around as if to piece together just why-the-heck he's sleeping in a chair. His brow knits at a third crowing. Groggily arising, he checks the time, then wobbles to the balcony doors. He pulls them open, then steps outside. In the dim light, he spots a rooster perched on a rusted wringer washer near the pink trailer. Carter winces as it crows again without the doors to muffle its intensity. "Oh geez," he comments painfully.

While rubbing his forehead, he leans heavily upon the railing and takes in the unusual sight. His eyes migrate toward the estate's gardens where a half-dozen goats munch away on the blossoms of Evelyn's precious hybrid roses. "Oh, not the damn roses," he complains.

Chapter Three

Please, Call Me Satan

With the sun now well above the eastern horizon, Carter steps out of the kitchen's French doors carrying his breakfast and coffee. He is dressed in the weekend sandals, khaki shorts and Hawaiian shirt that make him feel comfortable. The first sight to greet him on the patio is Mrs. Gilbert who is sprawled across two patio chairs, sound asleep and snoring like a lumberjack.

A disgusted grimace joins Carter's already annoyed expression. It is with similar repugnance that he surveys the rest of the patio with its mounds of blankets, towels, trash and remnants of food – which was not exactly his vision of breakfast on the patio.

He proceeds across the grounds to the tables near the pool where a film of grime and soap scum glistens atop the water. Puddles and freshly wet boy-size tracks leading the direction of the landslide initiate another slow burn. Carter disgustedly plops down at a table, deposits his meal, buries his head in his hands, and begins drawing and releasing long, slow breaths as these are purported to help diminish the likelihood of a stroke. At a point, he simply shakes his head, then having lost hope, mechanically begins to shovel his breakfast into his face. As he eats, he surveys the landslide that has buried his immaculate estate. At a point, a spark of resolve begins to glow in his eyes for Carter

Chatsblythe is not one to lose hope or give up or stroke out. When he finishes eating, he rises and strolls over to the mound.

"Hello," he calls with a tone lighter than his mood. "Young men. I'd like to speak with you." He gazes up and down the length of the mound, as he waits a response.

A rifle barrel appears, then the freshly washed teen with wet hair, wearing only skivvies, that holds it. "State yer business," Sausalito demands.

My business is a little get acquainted conversation. How would you and your brother…or possibly sister…I don't know, like to come down and talk?"

"State yer business."

"I just did," Carter answers a bit tersely. "I'd like you to come on down for a conversation."

"Don't reckon we'll be doin' that."

"Then how about I come up?"

"No tresspassin'," Cincinnati adds from behind a rifle barrel that appears beside his brother's.

Another slow burn begins. "Really?" Carter asks, then holds up his index finger. "I'll be right back." He winks, smiles, then heads back to the house.

Sausalito shrugs at Cincinnati who returns the shrug. Both disappear back into the shrubbery.

A few moments later, Carter steps out the French doors with an AK-47 slung over his shoulder, a 9mm pistol in a holster on his hip and a 12-gauge shotgun in his hands. He passes by Mrs. Gilbert who is still snoring away on the patio and heads directly toward the mound. He takes a position at the base of earth nearest the trailer, pumps the shotgun, and pops off a billion-decibel round in order to make himself known.

With a flail of her arms, Mrs. Gilbert falls off her chairs.

Atop the mound, goats scatter, chickens take flight and feathers fill the air.

The two boys, .22's in hand and britches now on, dash to the edge of the slide. With the smoking shotgun rested against his shoulder, Carter smiles pleasantly if not sincerely. "Good morning again. I've revamped my plan. I was wondering if you two boys wanted to play guns today. You know, maybe take pot-shots at each other. I'm thinking you go first because the game will pretty much be over after my turn."

The brothers look at each other, then look back at Carter.

"I didn't think so." Carter's artificially light tone changes to something a bit more dire. "I don't like having guns pointed at me so I don't want to see those pea-shooters again. Got it?" The boys nod and lower their weapons. "Good," he compliments. "I reckon I'm coming up there and I reckon we're going to talk. Do either of you have a problem with that?"

The boys look at one another, then back at Carter. Both shake their heads.

With a nod, Carter places his arsenal of guns on the grass. Wishing he'd worn hiking boots, he grabs hold of the exposed roots, raises a foot, and begins to climb. Struggling, but eventually coming atop the mound, he makes his way through bushes to enter the semicircle of rusted junk that surrounds the trailer. The two boys have leaned their rifles against the shack. Both are busily getting into their wet, but relatively clean shirts they just pulled off the clothesline. "You both look squeaky clean," Carter congratulates as he looks them over. "I hope your laundry came out okay."

An extra-large load of heavily soiled guilt washes over their faces.

"Excellent. You two can plan on spending at least a couple hours this morning helping our groundskeeper clean the pool. I realize you may not have much in the way of washing and bathing facilities, but my pool – and for that matter – my fountain – are not for bathing or washing clothes." Carter's eyebrow rises. "Understand?"

The boys nod compliance.

Carter relents with a kinder tone. "I'll hook you up with a cabana and my housekeeper will be glad to do your laundry for you."

The boys look at each other mystified, then back at Carter.

"A cabana is basically a bathroom," Carter explains, then takes a moment to look around at the junk and debris. "Quite the homestead you have here."

No response.

"Your place was up there?" Carter looks up the ravine, then curiously at a lone coyote that stands on the exposed hillside, fearlessly looking back at him. Carter continues a little distractedly. "We didn't know anyone lived up there. I take it you've been there for some time."

"All our lives," Sausalito answers, then also looks at the coyote. Sausalito nods his head. The coyote nods in return, then walks back into the rough.

After raising his eyebrow at the unusual exchange, Carter speculates, "You've seen all these homes built in this canyon then, haven't you?"

Sausalito nods.

"I bet you feel we're outsiders."

After another nod, Sausalito elaborates. "Used to be good huntin' down here. Deer, rabbits, fox. Even was a stream and beavers 'til the houses came." He halfway sneers at Carter. "Mama said it was progress and you can't get away from progress."

"Looks like you did your best."

"Yes sir."

"Hope you don't mind me asking, but was that your mother I saw you boys bury last night?"

A tear rolls down Cincinnati's cheek.

"Yes sir." Sausalito bites his lip.

"I'm very sorry."

The boys nod.

"Was she killed in the slide?"

Sausalito shakes his head. "The consumption. She's been ailin' a while."

"I'm sorry. You have any other family?"

A blank look from both boys is the only response.

"I see. That must be very difficult." Carter bites his lip, then adds a grimace to his expression as the awkwardness of the moment closes in. "I guess I should introduce myself. My name is Carter Chatsblythe. This," he gestures toward the mansion, "is my home."

"Sausalito Jones," the elder boy speaks, then nods his head toward his younger brother. "Cincinnati."

"Those are some interesting names."

The teen's humorless expression is followed with an equally humorless gesture toward the pink trailer. "This here's *our* home and you're standin' on *our* land."

"I see." Carter nods. "You boys realize we have a situation here?"

The boy nods.

"Things are going to get difficult. You and I need to get prepared for that. Mind if I ask your age?"

"Nearly seventeen," Sausalito answers and proudly puffs out the paltry collection of ribs that comprise his chest.

"Yeah," Carter observes sadly, "things are gonna get real difficult. I take it your family lived up there pretty much by your own ways."

"Yes sir. Mighty proud about that."

"You want to see where we buried our mama?" Cincinnati asks innocently.

"I'd like that very much." Carter attempts a convincing smile while the boy disobediently waves a hand at Sausalito's frown of disapproval.

"I picked the spot," the young boy offers as he leads the way down the path. Carter and Sausalito follow. They walk a short distance, then form a circle around the slightly mounded earth with the Eleanor Roosevelt rosebush now planted at its head.

Carter takes it in. "What is your mama's name?"

"Loretta," Sausalito answers. "As good a woman as ever walked this earth."

"I'm sure she was."

"You see the view of the fountain?" Cincinnati urges while pointing its direction.

"That's very nice." Carter looks back at the grave, then looks over at Sausalito and raises his eyebrows.

"We buried her on *our* land, so it ain't none a yer concern."

Carter nods. "Yeah, things are gonna get real difficult."

Sausalito suddenly looks toward the mansion with an expression of pure disgust. "You call the law on us?"

"Huh?" Carter asks dumbly, then turns to follow Sausalito's eyes.

A very disheveled Mrs. Gilbert is now standing on the patio with her arm raised to point out Carter and the boys to a police officer. "Oh geez," Carter sighs as the officer starts walking their direction. "I think my little shotgun demonstration might have awakened the neighbors." The officer gestures Carter and the boys down from the mound with a wave of his arm. "Folks around here like their peace and quiet." Carter looks at the boys sorrowfully. "You boys know what child welfare or social services are?"

Their blank looks are answer enough.

"You're about to find out." Carter starts walking back along the path. "Come on." The boys fall in behind him. "You're familiar with the government, I take it."

"Mama said it's of the Devil," Sausalito replies.

"Your mama makes a good point. But, the government makes the laws of the land and it's going to have real different ideas about how your living situation ought to look. I'm afraid you two going to be in the government's crosshairs in about three minutes time." As they come into the clearing around the trailer, they stop momentarily among the rusted junk. Carter asks, "Do you two go to school?"

"Mama handled our studies," Sausalito replies. "I gots me a plan to follow."

Carter looks at the pink trailer with its corrugated tin roof and skirting of weathered plywood and crumbled cinder blocks. He raises his eyebrows, then as he's shaking his head, begins to push his way through the bushes and make his way toward the edge of the landslide.

When Carter comes to the rim of the mound, the officer looks up from where he has been studying the arsenal of guns laying in the grass. When the boys come up to stand at Carter's side, a crease forms in the officer's brow.

"Crosshairs, boys," Carter says, then pitiably looks at the two ragged, orphan boys standing at his side.

A small army of police officers and child welfare workers have converged in the mansion's back yard. While the household staff dutifully cleans up the previous day's homeless camp on the patio, Carter sits under the shade of a large umbrella near his filthy pool where a slick of soap scum glistens in the morning sun. As he's sipping lemonade and watching everything from a distance, his cell phone rings. He looks at it, then answers. "Hello, Raymond. Thanks for calling back – Oh, fine, fine. Listen, I have a little problem over here at the house. – No. Amazingly it's not Evelyn this time. – I know that you don't necessarily do this sort of thing, but I'm wondering if you would be interested in representing a couple orphans that are in a difficult situation – Yeah, no parents, no family..."

Carter stops speaking when, from across the grounds, Sausalito's voice suddenly becomes loud. Carter stands and looks over at the group of officials who encircle the irate teen. Sausalito's arms are waving about wildly as he shouts at them. *"We ain't going nowhere! This here's our home! Ya'll need to quit harpin' on us and go mind yer own business! We's fine an' we can take care a areselves! I tol' ya'll, we's fine."*

"Yeah, Raymond, I'm going to need your help with this," Carter resumes. "These boys are a little different and by different, I mean that they're possibly from a previous century."

Carter squints. The boys are now frantically climbing up the tangle of roots toward their trailer with an officer climbing up after them in hot pursuit. "Listen, Ray," Carter stands and starts running toward the disturbance. "I got to go before they get their guns and bullets start flying through the canyon. – Alright, check your schedule and give me a call. I have to get going. Bye."

Unaware of anything but the previous afternoon's wine coolers that are now pounding inside her head, Evelyn gropes her way out of an upstairs doorway. She stumbles onto the balcony that overlooks the mansion's spectacular living room. Lurching toward the railing, step by painful step, she grabs hold of it, then begins to pull herself along. With hair that is grotesquely askew, wrinkles in her clothing that have nothing on the pillow lines pressed into her face, and unsteady limbs, she gingerly descends the winding staircase hand-over-hand. She hoarsely and only barely audibly calls, "Missus Gilbert. I need my tonic. Missus Gilbert. Missus Gilbert. Where are you, you old troll? Oh the pain. Oh the pain."

Sausalito is breathing heavily, his face is flushed, and his eyes are blazing as he watches the last of the officers and welfare workers depart from the grounds below his homestead. "They better be leavin'," he warns Carter. "An' if you pull any tricks on us you'll regret it."

Carter speaks in a soothing tone. "I'm not pulling any tricks on you. They're giving you until Monday to calm down and be reasonable."

"We's from feudin' stock," Sausalito continues to rant and wave his arms. "There'll be lead flyin' all over this valley if they come back talkin' orphanage, 'r group home, 'r foster home again. This here's our home an' we ain't leavin' it."

Carter is biting his lip white when Sausalito looks over at him. "You know what a lawyer is?" Carter asks.

Suspicion washes over Sausalito's face. "Mama said lawyers were of the Devil."

"Again, your mama makes a good point, but you're going to need one – and soon."

"Mama gots things arranged. I'm to talk to a lady at the bank first thing Monday for livin' expenses. We don't need us no lawyer. We got guns and we still got our home and we'll have us some money and we don't need us no lawyer for nothin'. We's jus' fine."

"You may think that, but I'm working on getting you a lawyer anyway."

"Don't reckon I'll be…"

"You're getting a lawyer."

Silence settles in as jaws set and lips tighten. Sausalito and Carter stare one another down. "Of the Devil," Sausalito mutters under his breath.

"Some are. Some aren't. I am good friends with this one and I can assure you that he is not of the Devil."

Sausalito leers at Carter. "This here's the U.S.A. We's sup'osed to be free to do what we want, when we want, how we want. Mama said so. It's our rights."

"At one time that might have been the case. Nowadays, in the U.S.A. you do what you're told when you're told to do it and you learn to be happy with football, television and celebrity gossip. Most of us are overweight, no one gives a crap, and neither you nor I have any real freedoms. They just let us think we do."

"Of the Devil."

"I don't disagree."

"We ain't goin' to no orphanage."

"Which is why I want to get you a lawyer. I see what you have here and what you had up there." Carter points up the canyon wall. "And whether you want to admit it or not, you see my predicament with what I have here and what's sitting in the middle of it."

Sausalito and Cincinnati look at one another.

"Listen," Carter begins anew. "We're neighbors and neighbors usually try to help each other out in times like these. If I invited you two for lunch today, would you come?"

As Sausalito purses his lips in contemplation, Cincinnati looks at his brother hopefully. "If it ain't no trick – *an' it better not be* – that'd be right neighborly of you."

41

When the shriek of a banshee – or more likely Evelyn – and let's not split hairs on this – pierces the air, Carter's eyes close with dread. He sighs. "I think my wife just discovered her roses." Goats start dashing about the grounds below as another piercing shriek begins. "Listen, you guys have got to build a pen for your goats or we're really gonna have some trouble on our hands." The boys look back at Carter – mostly clueless as to the direness of the situation.

Now wearing swimming trunks, Carter dives into the pool. Also in the pool are Sausalito and Cincinnati. They bob up and down in his waves as they cling onto the pool's side scrubbing the tile. After swimming to the bottom, Carter surfaces with a handful of the bottles Evelyn had tossed in the previous day. He swims over to the deck, lines them up, then goes back down for more.

"Missed a spot," Floyd gruffly directs from the opposite side of the pool. Cincinnati follows the direction of the old man's gnarled finger, turns back, then rescrubs a section.

"We was pretty dirty, huh, Sausalito?" Cincinnati asks his brother.

"We was," Sausalito agrees. "Can't dig no grave and not get dirty."

"I s'pose. I likes me this swimin' pool. The man said we can swim in it iffin we knows how an' we's clean an' we don't git areselves drowned."

While Sausalito sneers at his brother, Carter bobs up with a few more bottles. The teen glances toward him for a second, then turns back to his brother and whispers. "These ain't good people. We ain't gonna be swimmin' in their pool."

"We's swimmin' in it now," Cincinnati whispers back

42

hatefully, then swims around his brother to start scrubbing another section of tile. "You's always such a negative Nellie."

"These ain't our kind of people," Sausalito gripes back in a heated whisper.

"An' we ain't theirs but at least he's bein' nice to us and he even invited us to some fancy dinner after we pointed guns at him. He could'a just let those police take us away an' been done with us."

"That there's our land and our home. They can't do that. We got as much right to be here as them."

"Up there's our land and our home." Cincinnati points at the top of the ridge. "An' you know it."

Sausalito grunts, then turns away to scrub some more tiles.

The aroma of pizza baking in a stone oven wafts outside. A table set with seven places waits on the patio for all to sit down, eat together and get-acquainted.

With a dour, if not hateful expression, Evelyn positions a bottle of hand-sanitizer at every place on the table. She emits a groan of disgust every time she glances toward the boys who are still cleaning the pool. *"Be on good behavior."* Evelyn mocks with a curled lip. *"You gotta be nice to these boys. You gotta be nice to people in general, nah, nah, nah."* Evelyn sneers her husband's direction as he pulls himself out of the water, then stoops and extends a hand to pull the boys out as well. While they're drying off and beginning to get dressed, she tightens the generous pink chiffon tie of her sunbonnet that she has not-very-discreetly wrapped around her mouth and nose. "Ug," she shudders, rolls her eyes, then mutters to herself. "I can't believe he's invited those germ-infested hillbillies to lunch."

Mrs. Gilbert happens to be near enough with the salad

she brings to overhear the comment. She growls.

"They probably have fleas and lice," Evelyn defends. "You want to growl at me?" She blinks her hot pink, metallic-flecked irises. "You'll be growling when your skin is crawling with microscopic vermin and you catch the plague."

The housekeeper deposits the bowl on the table and looks with revulsion at the ghastly contact lens. "Aw, ya sissy. You're the one that makes me sick. How're you gonna eat pizza with that ridiculous crap wrapped around your face?"

"I'm not hungry. I'm only having a beverage," Evelyn retorts, then picks up a covered smoothie with a straw in it. She arrogantly demonstrates how she can maneuver the straw between the chiffon folds of fabric and then takes a sip. "Do you honestly think I'd touch anything those rodents came near?"

Mrs. Gilbert growls again and balls up a fist. "If the Mister didn't have us all on good behavior, I'd…"

Evelyn twists her face arrogantly at the threat, then plucks a pair of white cotton gloves from her pocket and pulls them over her hands. Then Evelyn takes a can of air-freshener from a different pocket, shakes it, and sprays a huge arc of *Springtime Bouquet* as Carter and the boys approach.

Carter narrows his eyes, flares his nostrils, glares at her through the settling mist, and clears his throat. "Evelyn, honey, I'd like you to officially meet our neighbors, Sausalito and Cincinnati Jones. Boys, this is my wife, Evelyn." While Evelyn smiles sweetly, she says nothing mostly because she's holding her breath and the two functions are mutually exclusive. She instead limply extends her gloved hand. With drawn and uncomfortable expressions, the boys study her hot-pink, sparkly eyes. One at a time, they take her dead-fish-like hand and shake it as best they can. Carter then points to Mrs. Gilbert. "And this is our housekeeper, Missus Gilbert."

As Evelyn turns and not-very-discreetly gasps for air, Mrs. Gilbert robustly thrusts her hand out and shakes the bejesus out of the boy's skinny little arms. "Those are some great names. Nice to meet ya'."

Evelyn daintily pulls the gloves off her hands and tosses them onto the patio. Mrs. Gilbert looks down at the gloves. When Evelyn looks defiantly at the housekeeper and sneers ever so subtly, Mrs. Gilbert growls again.

With the staff, Chatsblythes and boys now seated at the table, Carter picks up the pizza server. "Have you boys ever eaten pizza?" They look at him blankly. "Then you are in for a treat. Our Missus Gilbert is the best pizza-maker in the entire world."

"We seen pictures of pizza but we isn't sure 'bout eatin' it 'cause Mama says it's like eatin' cardboard an' it ain't real food." In spite of his comment, Cincinnati holds up his plate for a steaming slice – which he immediately touches, then blows on his stinging fingers.

Evelyn holds her breath and shields her face until the dispelled little boy germs have dissipated.

Sausalito accepts a slice on his plate, then examines it warily. Especially perplexed by the pepperoni – 'cause meat generally ain't round – he picks at it. "Is this here snake?"

Evelyn gags.

"That's pepperoni," Carter explains. "And we can discuss what it's made out of after we've eaten. But trust me on this; you'll like it."

The boys each peel off a slice of pepperoni, apprehensively taste it, then smile.

"Soda?" Mrs. Gilbert offers as she lifts a couple cans

into view.

"We likes us sodas." Cincinnati nearly leaps out of his seat to reach for one.

Judging by the boy's savage devouring, they have evidently warmed up to the idea of pizza. Bernard is as absorbed in observing their feeding frenzy as Evelyn is in avoiding the sight. Floyd, seemingly oblivious to anything around him, diligently gums his food, then leaves glistening pieces of soggy crust on his plate for all the world to enjoy. And lastly, Mrs. Gilbert eats like a Shop Vac set on high.

As the meal progresses, Evelyn discreetly and disdainfully begins to track Cincinnati's trails of spit and marinara goo from pizza-slice to veggie to dip to mouth to smeared glass to pant-leg and back. Fighting subdued revulsion, she eventually sets aside the smoothie she had been gingerly sipping but has now, oddly, lost the appetite for. Maneuvering a napkin between the wraps of chiffon, she delicately pats her lips, then glances up to find Cincinnati looking back at her.

"Ain't you hungry?" the boy asks.

With a wrinkle of her nose, Evelyn shakes her head microscopically, closes her eyes and lifts a nostril.

"What was that you was drinkin'?" the boy asks with food spraying from his mouth.

Fighting back another gag, Evelyn brings two fingers up to her lips and does not answer.

"Don't you talk?" the boy asks.

"Aw, she talks just fine. Most days you can't get her to shut up." Mrs. Gilbert replies in Evelyn's stead, scowls at her, sheepishly looks at Carter's disapproving expression, then goes back to sucking up and devouring everything in sight.

"My wife is feeling slightly ill today," Carter explains.

"We saw her drinkin' like a fish yesterday," Cincinnati casually observes. "Get it? Drinkin' like a fish? That's what Mama always said 'bout alcoholics." Then the boy whose teeth are covered in chewed food, smiles.

Evelyn turns away, holds one hand to her mouth and the other to her stomach.

"You know, I'd prefer you not rush to judgment about my wife's use of alcohol like that and perhaps," Carter suggests, "you could swallow what is in your mouth before you speak."

"Oh, sorry," Cincinnati replies, then slurps from his soda to wash the food from his mouth. When he smiles proudly, only half of his teeth are covered with soda-colored food goo.

Carter grimaces.

As the meal progresses, Cincinnati's glances toward Evelyn become more frequent. Although Evelyn tries to look anywhere but back at him, every accidentally returned glance garners a subsequent grin of food-covered teeth. Eventually, Cincinnati's glances become a lengthy stare. Catching her uncomfortably shifting eyes, he swallows a mouthful and speaks with dreamy amazement. "'Cept for yer pink eyes, you're the prettiest lady I ever seen."

Equally distressed and flattered by the comment, Evelyn looks at him oddly, then politely, but ever so slightly, smiles.

"Is you a movie star?" the boy asks. "You prob'ly got to be 'cause you're so pretty."

"Ohhhh," Evelyn melts. "That is sooo nice."

"An' you're even prettier when you smile. So, is you? A movie star?"

"I've modeled some," Evelyn explains as she vainly begins to unwrap pink chiffon from her face. She shakes out her hair. "I've never acted but I've been told I have the bone structure of a starlet from the classic period of..."

"You got the bone structure of the Crypt Keeper." Mrs. Gilbert's eyes roll up into her head and her lip tugs. "You need fifty pounds on ya." She turns to Cincinnati. "It's Mister Chatsblythe's business that provides all this." The surly housekeeper waves her hand dismissively at Evelyn. "She ain't no movie star."

Sausalito lowers his pizza and begins to sniff. Everyone's attention is drawn to him as he raises his head, continues to sniff, then turns toward the lawn. Spotting a rabbit, he freezes. His lip rises as he emits a low snarl. Sausalito very slowly sets the slice of pizza back on his plate and silently scoots his chair back. He stands, then crouches as he makes his way around the table. With all eyes on him, he steals ever-so-silently toward the rabbit.

"What is he doing?" Evelyn finally inquires.

Cincinnati holds a finger to his mouth and whispers. "He's huntin'."

Carter begins to chuckle, then whispers back, "Does he honestly think he's going to catch that rabbit?" Cincinnati points as Sausalito goes into a cat-like crouch. The rabbit nibbles on grass, oblivious to impending danger.

Suddenly, Sausalito springs – as does the rabbit. Both cut this way and that with lightening-fast turns. Blades of grass fly out from under Sausalito's rapidly churning boots like the spray of cuttings from a mower.

Then Sausalito leaps.

There is a shake of his head, a flash of fur – and it's over. He stands, straightens his clothing, then bends to gather up the rabbit by its hind legs. Every face at the table is wide-eyed and open-mouthed – except Cincinnati's. He licks his fingers and takes another bite of pizza.

Upon returning to the patio, Sausalito lays the dead

rabbit on an adjacent table, spits a wad of fur from his mouth, then picks a couple stray hairs from his lips with his fingers. He is wiping them off on his pants when he sits down at the table. Seeming not to notice the open mouths and stares, he picks up his pizza. Every eye is on him as he takes a bite, chews, then chases the mouthful with a slurp of soda. He curiously looks at the stunned expressions, then takes another bite and begins to chew. "Oh," he finally acknowledges, "sorry about not excusing myself."

Cincinnati leans around him to ask Carter, "So, what's your business?"

Carter looks back at the boy incredulously. "My business? You want to know what I do? I don't freaking believe what just happened."

"Oh, that?" Cincinnati questions. "He's pretty good, huh?" The boy licks his fingers, then leans forward for a carrot and a swath of dip. "These is good." He holds the carrot up, then gnaws away.

Carter asks Sausalito, "How are you able to do that?"

"Raised by wolves."

"No, he weren't." Cincinnati holds up his disgustingly slimy hand. "It was coyotes and only for two weeks one time when he wandered off back when I was still a baby."

"But they made me one of the pack – honorary member, Mama said." Excitement begins to build in Sausalito's voice. "When Ma'd let me run with 'em, or I could sneak off, they'd take me huntin'. Ran with 'em for years an' I learnt pretty good."

"But still, they wasn't wolves and the Devil'll git yer soul if you lie," Cincinnati admonishes. He turns to the others. "But you should see him wrassle a puma."

"I'll wrassle anything," Sausalito responds loudly, his eyes now wide and sparkling. "I wants to wrassle me a bear, but ain't none of those around no more." Sausalito shrugs, his eyes become dull, he shrugs again, then digs another slice of pizza from the tray. "What'd you say these was again?" he points at a topping.

"Artichoke," Carter answers.

One of the rear legs of the deceased rabbit lying on the adjacent table twitches.

Evelyn weakly brings one hand to her mouth and another to her stomach.

Observing her distress, Cincinnati gets up and walks to the adjacent table where he picks the rabbit up by the rear legs. He faces his brother and shakes the dead thing to accentuate his words. "Was you born in a barn? How many times did Mama tell you not to leave dead things on the table, 'specially in the kitchen or where we's eatin'?" He takes a few steps, then tosses the rabbit onto the lawn. It hits the grass with a dull thud, then rolls a couple times.

A small whimper emits from Evelyn's throat.

The boy wipes his hands on his pants before returning to the table. "Sorry about that. He ain't got no manners." The boy grabs hold of a couple pieces of pizza and rips one from the other. He positions the other slice back on the stone with a fingery pat. "This sure is good."

"I think," Evelyn says weakly, "I may go in and lie down." When she feebly begins to rise, Cincinnati abruptly stands and rushes to assist her. He quickly sucks his fingers clean, wipes them on his pants, and takes hold of her arm. "You ain't lookin' so good. I'll hep you." Evelyn's eyes roll up into her head, but lacking the strength and the will to argue, she numbly stumbles toward the door with the boy supporting her.

Laying in bed together under subdued lighting, Carter and Evelyn both look at the ceiling with eyes that cannot close. "I believe that was the most bizarre dinner I've ever

50

experienced," Evelyn comments.

"I'd have to agree with you on that." Carter nods. "I can still see Sausalito spitting fur out of his mouth."

"I can still see the dead rabbit hitting the lawn," Evelyn confides.

Carter laughs, then turns his head to look over at his wife. "Thanks for meeting them and letting them eat with us."

"Did I have a choice?" Evelyn turns to face her husband.

He shrugs. "You could have gone to your retreat."

"I've spent so much time there lately, it's getting old. Lunch was interesting. It'll make a good story if I can get anyone to believe me."

"I really am sorry about your birthday plans."

Evelyn shrugs. "Cass and I will do lunch tomorrow." She shrugs again, then forces a smile. "She's probably my only true friend anyway. Maybe big parties are a thing of the past."

"Maybe." Carter studies the woman lying beside him. "Remember your twenty seventh? The one we spent at base camp on Kilimanjaro?"

"I do," she replies with a glorious smile. "Just me and you."

"And five other hikers and seventeen guides," Carter adds with a laugh.

"Really? I only remember me and you." Evelyn's smile grows wider.

"You know, come to think of it, maybe it was just me and you." Carter smiles to catch a glimpse of the woman he married.

On a far wall of the suite are a series of portraits that end at age 29. Carter and Evelyn are: on the summit of Kilimanjaro, a dog sled at the North Pole, scuba diving in

The Great Barrier Reef, skydiving over the Alps, canoeing on the Amazon, riding elephants in India. In each picture, the sparkle in their eyes and the way they look at one another tell of an adventure beyond the locale.

Chapter Four

Looks of Adoration and Loathing

Sunday morning dawns with a bank of fog rolling along the canyon walls. Breaks in its aromatic waves promise the eventual arrival of a blue sky and warming sun. Carter and Evelyn nestle together in their luxurious bed. Somewhere outside, a rooster crows. Carter runs his finger along the curve of Evelyn's nose and the angles of her cheeks while she purrs.

"Happy birthday," he whispers softly. She smiles and squeezes him tightly. "Yer the prettiest lady I ever seen." He smiles.

She giggles.

The rooster crows.

"When you gonna learn to kill rabbits like that?" she questions with her best backwoods drawl. "Or wrassle bears? I wants me a real man fer muh birthday."

They laugh.

"You are beautiful." Carter nuzzles her hair, then nibbles her ear. She shivers and snuggles closer. "I might have to work my way up to bears," Carter admits. "Think I might wrassle me a puma today though – jus' fer fun."

The rooster crows.

"That'd be sweet. If you don't bloody it up too bad, I'd love a puma jacket," she muses.

"Well, I am an animal," he growls. The covers thrash.

She shrieks and laughs.

Mrs. Gilbert is done-up for church wearing stubby black high-heels, a calf-length skirt, matching jacket and a straw hat adorned with flowers. She steps from the kitchen out into the now beautiful sunny morning. In her hand is a covered plate. She sets it on a table that already has a decanter of juice and two glasses. She brings her fingers to her mouth and rips off a piercing whistle. In a moment, the distant sound of the screen door of the pink trailer banging against its jamb replies. A somewhat groggy-looking Sausalito appears at the edge of the slog a few seconds later. "I made ya' breakfast," she hollers. "Come an' git it while it's warm."

Sausalito nods and waves.

"I'll see ya' tomorrow." Mrs. Gilbert smiles, waves, then goes back into the mansion.

Upstairs in the master suite, Carter and Evelyn cuddle in a shaft of morning sunshine. Their open window allows the sound of Mrs. Gilbert's departing vehicle to filter in. "Could I interest you in a birthday breakfast?" Carter inquires.

"I'd adore a shortcake with blueberries and whipped cream."

"Then it shall be done, my lady."

"And strawberries."

"As you wish."

"I love Sundays, home alone and no servants."

"Me too." Carter rises, then searches for his boxers. Evelyn grabs her teddy from the floor. While she scoots off to the bathroom, Carter saunters to the window to look out on the landslide. "Still there," he comments to himself and shakes his head. He checks the time and picks up his cell phone. He dials and waits. "Raymond. Carter Chatsblythe here. Good morning. - Have you thought about my request? - I see. I have a standing tee-time at eleven at the club. If I kiss your old ass for nine holes and let you win, would you be able to come to a decision today?" Carter listens a moment, then laughs.

Evelyn comes out of the bathroom wearing one of Carter's shirts and a knowing smile. She walks close, then shouts toward the phone. "Don't fall for it, Raymond. He plans to *kick* your old ass for nine holes."

Carter turns from the phone. "Ray says happy birthday and mind your own business."

Smiling her bratty smile, Evelyn tries to pull some of Carter's chest hair. "Thank you, Raymond," she yells toward the phone. "I know he's lying about the 'mind your own business.' I'm twenty-nine again. Can you believe it?" She giggles loudly as Carter attempts to dodge her pinching fingers.

Carter then wraps his arm around her as much to subdue her as to embrace her. They stumble toward the door while he continues to speak to Raymond. "I'm buying your lunch and as many drinks as it takes to get you to agree to what I want. - Yeah, we had to cancel the party. You got her tweet on that, right? - I'll explain later. She's got her girlfriend coming over to take her out for dinner and only God knows what. Raymond, you will not believe what we have in the back yard." Carter and Evelyn start to descend the winding staircase. "No, you'll have to wait. I took some photos. See you at the club." He hangs up and turns to Evelyn. "What exactly are you and Cass planning?"

The couple playfully enters the kitchen with more interest in round two than food. Carter and Evelyn cavort around with laughter and hands grabbing. Both are completely unaware of Sausalito and Cincinnati watching them from the patio where they are seated mere inches outside the open French doors. The boys hold breakfast burritos in front of their open mouths while they stare at the frolicking couple. An, um, let's call it – educational moment – passes before Evelyn suddenly shrieks and steps behind Carter.

Carter turns toward the still open-mouthed boys with an equally surprised and uncertain expression. Cincinnati smiles to display food all over his teeth, then waves energetically.

Sausalito shakes his head with disgust and mutters disapprovingly, "Of the Devil."

The now much more subdued couple wears tightly wrapped robes as they eat their breakfast beneath at a table near the pool. "I am absolutely mortified," Evelyn complains while glaring toward the landslide. "I feel violated. Who knows what they saw."

Carter laughs good-naturedly. "They saw a beautiful woman and her husband doing what healthy couples do. Look at it this way, now they've had sex-education. I rather doubt that was on Loretta's lesson plan – bless her heart, rest in peace, whatever it is you say about the dearly departed."

"I'm glad you can laugh about it, but then it wasn't your body they were gawking at. I'll be so relieved when they're gone. I assume that's what you're bothering Raymond about on a Sunday morning. You have a whole staff of attorneys so I don't know why you're bothering him. We need to get those boys in a home – or possibly a zoo – and have that mess hauled away first thing Monday morning. I can't wait to get on with our lives."

Carter raises his eyebrows, but says nothing.

"Carter. What are you not telling me?"

"You know, this is your birthday, let's not talk about the landslide today."

"Carter…"

"Well fine, actually, I want to talk to Raymond about representing them."

"What? You're hiring *them* an attorney?"

"I think they need one." Carter squirms. "That's everything they have over there. That's their lives. If we have it all trucked away, it'll destroy them. Sausalito says that's their home and their land. In some ways, he's right."

"So you're telling me that if a tornado picks up a house and drops it somewhere, that's the rightful land it belongs on? That's ridiculous. You and I both know it doesn't work that way."

"They're eleven and sixteen. They were raised apart from society. Their idea of right and wrong is a lot more simplistic than ours."

"Not our problem. They need to blame their mother – may she rest in peace – for their ignorance. They've made it this long without her, they'll be okay."

Carter grimaces, says nothing, then raises his eyebrows a second time.

"Oh my gosh, Carter. What now?"

"It hasn't been all that long." Carter winces.

"What hasn't been all that long?"

"Their mother's death."

Evelyn blinks.

"They buried her Friday night – up there – on their land."

"Holy shit, Carter! You told me they were orphans and had been for a while. Now you're telling me she just died?"

"I know." Carter cringes.

"You mean to tell me she just died two days ago? And they actually buried her up there?" Evelyn points toward the mound with a stiff arm and an exquisitely polished nail.

"I guess she'd been ill for a while."

"So we have a corpse in the back yard. That's just great. Now I'm pissed."

"I didn't think you could handle much more with the staff revolting and the party being cancelled and the slide…"

"When are you going to treat me like an equal? I'm your wife – your other half – but you treat me like I'm a child or one of your possessions."

"I do not. Well, maybe the child part, but not the possession part. Did you really want to know that was what the hole was for? Would you *really* have wanted to know? I just didn't think you needed any more right then. I'm telling you now. Doesn't that count for anything?"

"Go to hell."

"Evelyn…"

"Now the filthy little hillbillies can see a healthy couple fight." Evelyn rises and storms toward the house.

"And you wonder why I don't tell you things," Carter yells after her.

Evelyn spins around with another pointing finger. "And quit trying to befriend them. They are *not* our neighbors, *not* our responsibility, *not* our friends, and they should *not* be eating their breakfast on *our* patio. I agreed to one, *one* meal and that was it. You better believe I'll be talking to *your* precious Missus Gilbert tomorrow. We do not feed vagrants."

Evelyn enters the house and promptly slams the door.

"That's just wonderful." Carter mutters to himself as he lowers his head into his hands. As an afterthought, he looks toward the slog where Sausalito stands near the edge peering back at him. With hard eyes, the teen turns, and after a couple long strides, disappears into the foliage.

Now dressed to kill or at least maim, Evelyn stands in the entry, a fabulous affair set off by the mansion's winding staircase and towering windows. She waits as the gates open and a bright yellow Porsche Carrera 911 with its top down zips into the driveway and screeches to a stop near the front steps. Evelyn pulls open the mansion's doors, steps forward, flips her hair back and poses elegantly. Her effort is wasted as Cass, a tall, full-figured, gorgeous woman opens her car door, stands, then pulls down her large, bejeweled sunglasses to look at the monstrous slide that protrudes beyond the mansion. "Evelyn," she begins cautiously, "what is that?"

Evelyn re-strikes her pose and re-flips her hair, waiting to be noticed.

Again, the effort is wasted as Cass closes the car door. Never taking her eyes from the mound of earth, she begins to walk toward it.

Evelyn abandons the well-framed first impression to march outside and join her friend – who now walks on the grass as if she is being pulled into the slide's field of gravity. After pulling off her stiletto heels, Evelyn rushes to catch up. "Cass. *Cass!* Could you wait up?"

Cass finally stops and turns toward Evelyn who is awkwardly tiptoeing across the lawn toward her. Cass looks her up and down. "You look nice," she acknowledges with a matter-of-fact tone.

"Nice? I look nice? This," Evelyn waves her hands at herself, "took two hours of preparation."

"Seriously?" Cass asks with one eyebrow raised. "Two whole hours? I was thinking somewhere in the range of ten minutes."

"Sometimes I really hate you."

"You do not. I'll assume what you meant to say was: Cass, you look absolutely fabulous!" Cass flips her hair and strikes a pose. "Because I always do."

"Ahhhhh!"

Cass laughs as she hugs her rigid friend. "I know you wanted me to look at you, but Evelyn, what the hell is this? Oh, and happy birthday, sweetie." She kisses her.

"That's the reason I had to cancel the party." Evelyn glowers at the mound of earth. "And probably the impetus for my impending divorce."

"Oh, Evelyn. You know poverty isn't your color." Cass resumes her curious stroll into the pull of planet mud. With Evelyn at her side, she comes around the corner of the mansion to behold the entirety of it. "I cannot believe this. This is amazing."

"Just wait 'til you hear what Carter's up to…" Evelyn complains.

"Is that a trailer on top of it?" Cass squints at the pink hillbilly homestead that is glistening in the sunlight.

"Complete with hillbillies. You won't believe…"

"A pink trailer. I've always wanted one of those. Is it going to be a guest house?"

"I hate you. I really hate you."

"I love you too, darling. Is this the most bizarre thing ever? Why didn't you tell me? I heard about a landslide a couple days ago on the news. I had no idea it was in your yard – unless of course this is some kind of performance art you hired done for your birthday."

"I'm glad you find my pain amusing."

"I always have." Cass looks back up at the trailer. "Are people actually living in that?"

"Not real people like you and I. There are two of the dirtiest little man-child whatevers you've ever seen holed

60

up in that piece of crap. Can we go? If the filthy little one sees I'm here, he'll come out and stare at me. He – they – essentially saw me naked this morning. I am so mortified. Can we go?"

"Naked, huh? They probably thought you were another boy. I'll have to tell them you aren't."

"You are just hilarious."

"Hello," Cass suddenly shouts up at the trailer.

"No. Stop that."

"Hello? Hello?" Cass yells louder.

Cincinnati comes running to the edge of the mound shirtless, looks around, then spots them. As Evelyn turns away with a hand held to shield her face, Cass breaks a wide smile. "Well, hello there handsome! Aren't you just adorable? Would you look at you?"

After looking down at his bony ribs, bare stomach, ratty jeans and frayed boots for a moment, Cincinnati looks back up, perplexed.

"You are just the cutest little thing," Cass gushes.

"Could. We. Go?" Evelyn growls through gritted teeth with her face turned and eyes averted.

"We have plenty of time." Cass waves her hand. "Our reservation isn't until one." Cass looks back up at the boy. "I want one."

"You can have that one. And his brother. And their chickens and their goats. I'll have them and their pink trailer trucked over to you. I can't be here. I'll be waiting for you out front." When Evelyn skulks away, Cass glances at her departure only momentarily before her attention returns to the boy.

"Hi, I'm Cass. What's your name?"

"Cincinnati."

"You're kidding. Cincinnati? As in Ohio? Really?"

"Mama liked the sound of it."

"Then I'd have to say your mama has remarkably good taste."

The boy smiles. There is a rustle in the greenery and Sausalito appears. He is dressed approximately the same as his brother but with a very grim expression. He looks at the beautiful well-dressed woman with contempt. Then with a sneer, takes his brother by the arm and begins to pull him away.

"Well, look-e-you!" Cass feigns lusty astonishment. "What a handsome little piece a man you are."

Sausalito's sneer morphs into a questioning look.

When Cass winks with comical exaggeration, Sausalito cannot help but smile.

"Oh my goodness. Would you look at that smile? I'm gonna come up there and eat you."

"She's gonna eat you," Cincinnati laughs. Although Sausalito's confusion deepens, his smile broadens.

Still looking up at Sausalito, Cass asks, "What do they call you, besides absolutely gorgeous?"

After another embarrassed and shy smile, Sausalito answers, "Sausalito, Ma'am."

"Sausalito Ma'am? Now *that* is a peculiar name."

While Cincinnati laughs, Sausalito reiterates humorlessly, "Sausalito. Ma'am."

"Ohhhhh. You know, I probably knew that. I was making a joke. That is a fabulous name."

Sausalito looks at her uncertainly.

"So, it's just you two up there?"

"Yes ma'am."

"Would you quit with the ma'am crap? Call me Cass. In fact, you can call me anything, but don't call me late to dinner." She laughs and slaps her abundant thigh.

The boys look at her.

She closes her eyes and shakes her head. "Once again,

it was humor. We'll work on it." She looks more intently at the boys, then becomes subdued. "I have never seen two more fine-looking young men in all my life. I am so glad to meet you. But speaking of late to dinner, Miss Persnickety will have a fit if I dally too long. I'll look forward to getting to know you two better some other time." Cass winks at the boys and blows them a kiss. "This is just the most remarkable thing. Amazing." She heads back across the lawn with a final wave goodbye.

Chapter Five

Burglars and Angels

With Carter gone golfing in a plan to extort Raymond's compliance, Evelyn at lunch, and no servants in the mansion, Cincinnati and Sausalito freely roam about the grounds investigating their new and very opulent surroundings. While Cincinnati curiously examines, feels and climbs on everything, Sausalito's enthusiasm is slightly more guarded. Glowering above his tightly folded arms, he follows his little brother who is at present heading toward the pool. Obviously keeping a lookout with his many uncomfortable glances around, he mutters, "You know they gots cameras everywhere and they're gonna see us snooping around."

"So what?" Cincinnati shrugs. "We ain't hurting nothin'." He runs to stand beside a statue, then mimics its pose and dead expression. With no laugh forthcoming from his brother, he gives it up and goes to kneel at the pool. He runs his hand in the water. "It's so warm. When can we go swimmin' fer fun?"

"We ain't gonna be swimmin'. That there lady don't want us here. Come tomorrow, I'll bet you the police will come and take us away."

"Nuh-uh." Cincinnati stands. "Let's go look in their windows." With Sausalito trudging after, Cincinnati excitedly heads toward the house.

"You'll see tomorrow," Sausalito warns. "We should pack and go back up on the ridge where we belong."

"Mama put us here for a reason. This is where our home is so here's where we belong. You said it yerself, Mama did some powerful work afore she left us."

"Maybe it was a test, to see if we'd stay true to our ways."

Sausalito's words are ignored as Cincinnati cups his hands, then presses them and his face to a window. "What would we live in?" is Cincinnati's belated response.

"We got tarps. We can build us a tent."

"I ain't livin' in no tent. Mama'd have a fit. The man said he was getting us a lawyer to look out for us."

"People like them lie. You can't trust 'em. If there's a lawyer, it's for him."

"What do you suppose all this stuff in this room is for?"

Sausalito unfolds his arms, cups his hands and looks in the window.

"That's exercise equipment. This here's their gym."

"These people are super-rich, huh?"

Sausalito growls, "These people are of the Devil."

"Mama said people was never of the Devil 'cause they're made by God. Only the things people *do* is of the Devil 'cause the Devil gits into people sometimes."

Sausalito gestures around them. "This here is of the Devil."

Cincinnati makes a face. "I don't think it's bad."

"Mama said…"

"Mama said I should think for myself."

Sausalito trudges after Cincinnati as he goes to another window.

"Whoa! Look it this," the boy exclaims.

Sausalito cups his hands, then peers through the glass.

"Whoa."

"This must be the living-room, huh?"

"I'd say. I never seen nothin' like this."

"Me neither. That's a whole acre big and two stories high." Cincinnati pulls himself away from the window with his face now glowing. "I wanna go in."

"It ain't a acre big and they ain't never gonna invite you in. That lady…"

"Who said anything about a invitation?" Cincinnati grins deviously, then runs for the series of French doors that run along the kitchen.

"Young'un," Sausalito warns as he dashes after his brother, "I will put you over my knee."

"Won't neither. I'm too big an' I'll give you a black-eye." The boy tries door after door – eventually finding one left unlocked. His eyes grow large when the latch clicks open. He turns toward his brother's scowl.

"They's got them burglar alarms," Sausalito warns. "You open that and bells and sirens will go off jus' like in the mystery stories we read."

"What if a breeze comes along and…" Cincinnati pushes the door open and nothing happens.

"It's prob'ly a silent alarm and the cops is on their way. We gotta go." Sausalito grabs his brother by the arm and begins to pull.

Cincinnati tugs out of his grip and faces him with a scowl of his own. "You sure is a nervous Nellie. Mama always said you's high-strung. We ain't hurtin' nothin'. Why can't we look around? They have all this 'cause they want people to see it."

"What if they come home and catch us?"

"You can stand out front and whistle if they come but I'm goin' in."

"Young'un. I swear I'll discipline you."

66

"Gotta catch me first," Cincinnati dares, then dashes inside the house.

After cautiously looking around the vacant yard and not hearing sirens, Sausalito also ventures in. Cincinnati stands in the middle of the living room looking up at a hand-painted ceiling bordered with ornately carved gilded trim. His mouth hangs open as he slowly turns circles to take it in. "This here's like that place in Rome that Mama showed us pictures of."

His brother rigidly approaches but gazes around at the staircase and balconies. "The Sistine Chapel is what you's talkin' about. Well, now you seen it so we gotta go."

"There's gotta be a hunderd rooms. I ain't even started."

"That's it," Sausalito yells. The chase is on as Cincinnati takes off for the staircase. They thunder up the stairs in the quiet home with Cincinnati screaming in panic.

"Young'un," Sausalito threatens, "you best stop. I'm gonna whup yer ass."

The boy clears the stairs, then opens the first door he comes across, ducks in and quickly slams it. While he struggles to figure out the lock, Sausalito's much stronger hand grabs the knob. Even if Cincinnati pushes against the door with all his might, big brother gradually begins to power it open. When Cincinnati is forced to abandon the contest and step aside, Sausalito stumbles inside and the door slams back against the wall.

Now having abandoned the battle, both boys are stopped in their tracks by the sight that greets them. Most striking is the sheer number of finely-dressed and posed dolls. Hundreds of dolls of every color and size, boys and girls, seated, hugging, having tea, walking, bending, reclining on shelves and posed in dioramas encompass the entire suite. Both boys look about with open mouths. In the center of the room sits an ornate canopy bed draped with covers of satin and lace. Hanging below the canopy are angels of every size and shape – dolls with sparkling wings and flowing robes of white – in flight with eyes cast heavenward, or with benevolent faces looking downward. Hands either rise to Heaven or reach down to help. Aside from the breaths of the boys, it is completely silent.

"Lord Almighty," Sausalito finally comments.

"Ain't never seen nothin' like this," Cincinnati concurs. "Is this here a museum?"

"Don't rightly know."

"It ain't of the Devil." The boy looks around. "That's for sure."

"It's like Heaven," Sausalito ponders. "Mama should'a died in a place like this – not on the floor of our crappy ol' trailer."

The young boy begins to walk on carpet deep and soft and white as a cloud. He goes to the bed where he peers up at the angels. "Look, there's clouds and rainbows and beams of light painted up inside this thing here."

Sausalito goes to the canopy and looks inside, perhaps marveling more at the carpet his feet sink into than the sight before his eyes. He bounces on the carpet and shifts his weight while he looks at the heavenly scene above. The ivory satin comforter draws his hands onto it. The brothers begin to push and prod, feeling the softness. "Lord Almighty," Sausalito repeats, then looks upward again. "Young'un, that there ain't painted. That's what they call three-dimensional – see how that's lumpy and all? And that there's embroidery, not paint. I think it's silk or something."

Cincinnati peers at it. "Lord Almighty. These people are rich."

"That they is."

Cincinnati walks over to a shelf and touches a doll with a porcelain face and lace dress. "Do these people have them a little girl?"

Sausalito draws up to his bother's side. "Don't know."

"Maybe she died. Maybe this was her room an' she died right here and that's why there's angels all around."

"Don't know."

"I hope no one died in here."

"There ain't no pictures a anyone, so prob'ly not."

"Huh," Cincinnati ponders. "Maybe there's a boy's room here somewhere too with cars and trains on shelves and planes hanging from the ceiling. That would be so neat."

Sausalito nods thoughtfully as he looks at his brother's wide, excited eyes. "Might be." He then reaches out quick as a whip to grab Cincinnati's collar. "Yer snoopin' days is over."

"Noooo!" Cincinnati squirms desperately as he tries to tug away. As he is dragged across the carpet, he manages to reach out and grab one of the balusters on the bed.

"Young'un. I am warnin' you."

The boy's other hand latches on to the post as well. "I jus' wanna look at stuff. I ain't hurtin' nothin'."

All of a sudden, the boy is picked up around his waist and hoisted onto big brother's shoulder. His hands hold tight but his mouth is open wide and screaming. Big brother picks at Cincinnati's white-knuckled fingers, trying to remove them from the baluster – mostly in vain.

With the commotion, neither hears the guttural throbbing of the Ferrari as it pulls into the driveway and comes to a stop just outside the front doors. And of course they would not have heard Raymond's sedate black Mercedes sedan pull in behind it.

Giving up on plan 'A', Sausalito sets his screaming

brother down, pulls back his hand, then begins to swat the boy's butt. "Owwwww," Cincinnati cries. "Would you quit... Ooowww! Stop it." Cincinnati twists around trying to evade his brother's hand while keeping both of his latched onto the post. Suddenly both hands leave the post to protect his butt. In an instant, long skinny arms bear-hug him. With his arms clamped to his side, Cincinnati resorts to screaming bloody murder as he's transported toward the door. *"Noooo..."*

Raymond Bartel, an older white-haired gentleman wearing vintage golf attire, accompanied by Carter, who is dressed in more contemporary clothing, have come together near the front steps of the mansion with their eyes focused on the slog of earth that protrudes beyond the side of the house.

"Well, I'll be," Raymond marvels. "Had that come twenty feet this way, your home would've been a pile of rubble."

"It would have done a number on it," Carter agrees, then inclines an ear toward the front door. "Did you hear that?"

Raymond shrugs. "Hear what?"

Carter begins to ascend the steps. "Sounds like wild animals in there..." He readies his key while hastening to the door.

Inside the doll room, Cincinnati has yet to concede defeat and has both feet planted of either side of the door his brother is attempting to push him through. He is still screaming his lungs out when suddenly, Sausalito spins around and pulls him through the door instead. Once outside the doll room, the boy continues his futile thrashing in Sausalito's unrelenting grip and screams as if

70

he was being murdered. Sausalito makes his way along the balcony and is about to descend the staircase when the front door opens. Like the earlier sounds of vehicles arriving, it goes unnoticed.

Carter is nothing less than mortified as he watches Sausalito carry the screaming, squirming boy down the steps. "Boy, when I git you home I am gonna give you something to scream about. I am gonna welt yer hide."

When the boys come around the curve of the staircase, Cincinnati's wild eyes land on Carter first, then on Raymond as the stunned older gentleman, draws up to Carter's side.

He suddenly becomes silent.

"I cannot believe the way yer actin'. Mama would be so ashamed…" Sausalito pauses, actually hearing himself speak, then follows his brother's gaze. When he sees the two men standing at the foot of the steps, he becomes still. A second later, he sets Cincinnati down on the stairs. Both boys stand there panting.

Carter pulls his mouth closed. Flared nostrils, narrowed eyes and a firmly-set jaw follow.

Sausalito shakes his head and covers his face with both hands. "I tol' you this would happen." Then taking his hands away, he speaks to Carter. "I am real sorry. He…"

Carter holds up a hand to silence him. While the boys catch their breath, Carter takes a couple deep breaths to calm himself. After a moment, he cups his hand at the boys to gesture them down the staircase.

As Sausalito walks down the steps, he looks between Carter and Raymond as he speaks. "I apologize for us bein' in your home like this. I know it ain't right. It won't happen again."

Carter manages a hard swallow.

In the ensuing silence, Cincinnati timidly begins, "This

71

here was my fault. I came in yer house and all my brother did was try to stop me. I only wanted to see stuff. I didn't mean no harm. I just ain't never seen nothin' like this before. It's so beautiful."

Carter's hands go to his hips. He looks away and flexes his jaw as he slowly shakes his head.

"Mama always said I could be a handful." The boy attempts an ingratiating smile.

Carter rolls his eyes and continues to shake his head.

"We'll be on our way." Sausalito places a hand on his brother's shoulder and begins to guide him toward the door.

They get no more than a couple steps before Carter sighs loudly. The boys turn back. "Boys, this is Raymond Bartel. He'll be your attorney." With a disgusted incline of his head, Carter nods toward the elder boy. "Sausalito." Then he introduces the younger with a similar nod. "Cincinnati."

Raymond steps forward with his hand extended. "Pleased to meet you." The three shake hands as Carter watches.

"I'm taking a shower," Carter announces. "You do what you need to do." He turns away and sets one foot on the stairs.

"Sir?" Sausalito's voice stops him momentarily. "Thank you."

Without turning, Carter closes his eyes. He nods, then continues up the steps.

Chapter Six

I'm Gonna Draw Me a Picture

The afternoon sun draws near the ridge as Carter swims laps in the pool, pausing occasionally to hang on the side where he sips from an icy glass of lemonade. As he's bobbing in the water his eyes are drawn to the landslide time and again where the boys sit in the shade of a few dwarf trees near their mother's grave. Occasionally his and their curious glances intersect before he plunges back into the water to continue his swim.

As Carter begins another series of laps, Cincinnati ventures, "I sure would likes me to swim."

"Even if the lady would'a let you – *an' she wouldn't* – I think yer earlier stunt kinda ruined any possibility of that." Sausalito also watches Carter a moment, then faces his brother. "I need me some time to think. That lawyer man said we got real problems. What you say we hike up the ridge and look around at what's left of the old place? We ain't been up there since all this happened."

"I su'pose we could." The boy gazes at the pool. "I think he'd let us swim even after what I done."

"Young'un, you think the world is all sunshine and roses. It ain't. I tol' you, we got us some real problems here."

"But the mister lawyer man said he's gonna help us."

"He said he's gonna *try*. He said it ain't lookin' so good

for us an' I still ain't sure about lettin' him."

"I know." The boy ponders a bit. "Do you trust him?"

Big brother shrugs. "He knows a lot. Says he's country boy at heart. I jus' looked at him like he was a liar. He don't look like no country boy to me an' I ain't stupid. Think he's tryin' to butter us up." He frowns. "I think if we go back up our hill, things might go back the way it was. No one knew we's up there and ain't no one gonna bother to go up there to git us. Might be simple as that."

"What about Mama and our place here?"

Sausalito shrugs. "Don't know. Let's go on up. I kin prob'ly think clearer up there. Maybe somethin'll come to me."

"Or me. I gets me pretty good ideas."

"Yeah. Er you." Sausalito rises and stretches out the cricks from sitting. He glances toward the pool where Carter hangs on the edge once again sipping lemonade. Cincinnati rises as well and comes up to his brother's side. They both look at Carter. "You wanna fetch us some hikin' water?" Sausalito asks. "I'll wait fir ya."

"We's almost outta water."

"Yeah, I know. If they'll still let us use the cabanas, we'll fill us some jugs tonight after they's gone to bed."

While Cincinnati heads back on the trail that leads toward the trailer, Sausalito returns his attention to the pool. Carter nods with a backward tilt of his head. Sausalito returns the nod. After slipping back in the water, Carter swims only a couple strokes, then comes up and takes hold of the edge of the pool. He hoists himself up and shakes the water out of his hair. Then looking purposefully at Sausalito, he holds up a finger and begins to walk his way. About the time he makes it to the base of the slog, Cincinnati returns with a glass jug of water. They all look apprehensively at one another.

74

"I thought we might talk a minute," Carter begins.

The boys look at one another, then back at him. "I tol' you we was sorry about us being in yer house," Sausalito offers.

"I understand you were actually trying to do the right thing. I like you two boys so I don't want things to be tense between us over that one incident."

After another look is exchanged between the boys, Sausalito nods. "I appreciate that."

"Listen," Carter begins. "Let's keep all of what happened about you two being in the house between us. Evelyn would freak out if she heard you were in there. That room you boys went into is her special place."

"Yeah. We thought that," Sausalito nods. "We's sorry about yer little girl."

"My little girl?"

"The one that died," Cincinnati clarifies.

"Ummmm," with squinted eyes and a crease in his forehead, Carter considers the boy's utterly sincere expressions. Then his face smoothes and he exhales. "Ohhh, the dolls. No. No, those are *Evelyn's* dolls."

The boys look at one another with the same perplexed expression that just left Carter's face. "Why does she gots dolls?" Sausalito asks.

"She needs the world to be perfect."

"But they's dolls," Cincinnati argues.

Carter shrugs. "They comfort her when life gets difficult."

"She gots ever' thing in the whole damn world," Sausalito bursts. "When is life difficult?"

"It's hard to explain." Carter shrugs again.

"Lord almighty," Sausalito scoffs.

"I hear ya, but listen, she can't know you were in there. She'd feel even more violated than she already does after the – you know – um – morning incident."

"We won't say nothin'," Sausalito assures Carter. "She don't like us no-how and I's smart enough to know that'd make it worse."

"You know, it isn't that she doesn't like you. She's just embarrassed about what you saw this morning."

When Cincinnati smiles luridly, Sausalito frowns at him and delivers an elbow to his side.

Carter clears his throat. "So you can understand why she's embarrassed."

Cincinnati grins some more.

"Listen, you can't let her know you saw anything – you know – of her – you know," Carter cautions.

"Think she knows we did. She ain't stupid," Sausalito bluntly states.

"No. She isn't."

"She's real pretty," Cincinnati says with a goofy smile spreading across his face. "I didn't know girls looked like that. Never would've thunk it neither."

Carter closes his eyes and shakes his head but cannot conceal his blush. "Yeah. It's things like that that make it difficult. No one's fault, just, you know, it happened and now we have to find a way to deal with it."

"I'm drawin' me a picture," Cincinnati boasts with his goofy smile returning to his face.

"Oh dear God," Carter laments.

"Tol' him I didn't think it was decent." Sausalito agrees. "I'll be sure it gits burnt if'in he does."

"I'd appreciate that." Carter thinks a moment. "How did things go with Raymond?"

Sausalito shrugs. "Went okay. He mostly just asked a bunch a questions. Says we need to talk more 'fore anyone does anything. Tells us to stay put and don't talk to no one. Says he'll speak for us but I ain't so sure about that."

Carter nods. "I know you didn't want a lawyer. You think he'll be all right?"

A shrug. "Told him we'd think about acceptin' his help."

"He's a good man." Carter looks at the jug of water. "You boys about to go somewhere?"

With an incline of his head, Sausalito explains, "We's about to hike up where we used to live. See how it is after the slide."

Carter nods.

"Ain't seen yer wife lately," Sausalito leads.

"She's out for dinner and a movie with her friend. She'll be gone until this evening. This piece of land sliding down here like it did saved me thousands for the party she was planning."

"Thousands a what?"

"Dollars."

"You was gonna spend thousands of dollars on a party," Cincinnati nearly yells.

Carter shrugs.

"Lord almighty," Cincinnati exclaims.

"Of the Devil," Sausalito comments to himself.

"Getting a little tired of hearing that," Carter responds. The look he and Sausalito exchange seems to indicate that they don't agree not to agree.

The following Monday morning dawns peacefully upon the estate. Raymond's black Mercedes sits in the driveway with the first rays of sun reflecting off its shiny contours. Floyd pokes around the grounds in the cool of the day. Atop the landslide, a rooster is perched on a rusted wringer-washing machine near the pink trailer. It crows. The blinds and curtains of the mansion are still closed. Wearing boots, jeans and a flannel shirt, Raymond sits alone atop the mound at the boy's picnic table. His hands are clasped upon an old photo album set before him. Through the open windows of the trailer, he listens to the first stirrings and raspy voices of the boys as they awaken from their slumbers. As he watches the rooster move about on the washer, the voices inside the trailer, interspersed with bouts of coughing and the clearing of throats, get louder. He waits.

Footfalls upon the creaking floor become more active just before the door opens. "It weren't like that yesterday," Cincinnati complains from the dark interior.

"I know," Sausalito replies. "I heard things poppin' and groanin' last night. Earth is settlin'. We prob'ly got to start jackin' and shorin' up to get the trailer level again."

The spring on the screen door complains as it is pushed open. Ratty boots step down on rickety steps. Sausalito's eyes almost immediately land upon Raymond. His lips purse and his eyes squint, but he continues out the door and off the steps with Cincinnati following. Both boys then stop and stand staring at Raymond. "Good morning," the old man says.

"Mornin'," is Sausalito's terse, and very guarded response.

"I'm here to talk. Thought I'd catch you bright and early. I imagine you're fixin' to do some business. I'll wait."

The boys nod uncomfortably, then walk into the shrubbery. As they're taking a leak, Cincinnati whispers, "What's he want to talk about?"

"Don't know. Think he's playin' dress-up to git us off our guard. Rich folk don't dress like that. Don't believe nothin' he says an' let me answer his questions. He thinks we's stupid."

"Want me to fetch my gun an' run him off?" Cincinnati asks while zipping up his fly.

"We'll hear him out first but if I give you the signal, go git yer gun." Sausalito finishes laying out his plan, then covers his stomach with his hand. "Don't feel so good today. I'm thinkin' after we run him off, we pack up and head up the hill fer good."

Although Cincinnati's expression seems not to relish the thought, he nods.

The rooster crows, then flaps its wings. It flies off the washer as the boys return to the clearing, pecks at something on the ground, struts around importantly, and crows some more. Raymond gestures to the bench opposite him, then waits while Sausalito approaches and sits. Cincinnati remains standing. The teen and Raymond look at one another a moment before Raymond unclasps his hands, then pats the photo album in front of him.

"Thought you might like to see where I come from. I was thinking after we spoke yesterday that you might have thought I'm not your kind of people. I know that's important to folks like you and I. Thought I might be able to put your mind a little more at ease if you knew a little of my history." The elderly man opens the antique brown embossed cover to reveal pages of black and white photographs. He turns the book so that it's right-side-up for the boys. The finger of his spotted hand points to a young boy standing amidst a group of farmers that are wearing bib-overalls and women dressed in aprons that are surrounded by raggedy children. "This is me, age nine back in nineteen-forty-seven."

The boys peer at the image.

"Sharecroppers. That's what we were. See this shack over here?" Raymond points at another photo. "This is where we lived. No running water. No toilet. We had electricity so we had lights and a radio. Also had a wind-up Victrola. Wasn't much, but we thought we had it all." He turns the page. "Here's me with my twenty-two and my brother. We'd go out in the fields and shoot what we could find and that's what the family ate. We drove a twenty-nine Chevrolet when it ran and we had money for petrol." His finger moves to another photo. "This is my mom and my pop – last photo together. She lived to the ripe old age of forty-three and him to sixty-two. Good people. Had nothin'. Good people." Raymond nods nostalgically. "God love 'em." He turns a page. "This is me the day I enlisted for the army. Served the good old U.S.A. My family was mighty proud." He rapidly turns a few pages. "Here I am, probably fifteen. These aren't in order. Guess I'm five or so in this one. Check the long hair on me there." He stops. "You see anything here where I had anything? You see anything here to say I wasn't a country boy?"

Sausalito's dull eyes examine the old man's face. "No sir."

"I was every bit what you and your brother are. Every bit. Would I go back to the way I lived? No sir, I would not. Do I love that it made me who I am? Yes sir, I do. Do I long for simpler times and better ways and maybe a pot of greens every now and then? You bet I do.

"I got out. Turned out I was smart. I didn't know the ways of the world but I learned them and I made myself a life. I brought these pictures to show you it can be done. It's okay to change and still be true to who you are.

"Now I'm not here because I don't have anything better to do and I'm not here because Carter asked me for a favor. I'm here because you don't know the ways of the world any more than I did way back then. Today the world is a thousand times more complicated than it ever was for me. I know you're thinking about letting me help you. Whether you know it or not, you need help. I know you're mourning the loss of your mother. That's a lot. But time isn't going to wait on you to come to a place where you're ready to deal with it. It's here and unfortunately it's today.

"Carter's got the authorities crawling all over him about this hunk of earth in his yard and you two boys living in this trailer. If the authorities get their way, you boys are going into foster care and your home is going into a landfill. Your mama is going to be dug up and an autopsy done on her. Then she'll be buried twenty miles from here in a pauper's cemetery. Is that what you want?"

"I ain't gonna let that happen," Sausalito defiantly states.

Leaning close to the youth, Raymond speaks very clearly. "You won't have any choice. You are sixteen years old."

The boys look at one another. The rooster crows. A slight breeze drifts their way, bringing with it a foul odor. Wincing at the scent, Raymond turns away as he covers his nose. "Good Lord, did something die over there?"

"We smelt it all night," Cincinnati offers. "We's thinkin' something crawled under the trailer and died."

"Yeah," Sausalito confirms. "We don't feel so good. Kept the windows open but it barely helped." He looks between his brother and Raymond. "Mama said I gotta go to the bank this morning and talk to a lady. I got papers to show her."

"I thought we agreed that you would wait. I'd like to look at those papers before you talk to anyone," Raymond insists as forcefully as he thinks he can.

The boys share a glance. After looking again at the photo album, Sausalito purses his lips, looks at his brother, then rises. He walks to an old cook stove that sits indiscriminately amongst the junk and kneels to open the door. After pulling out a tin box, he rises, then goes back to the table. "This here is everything important Mama said to keep."

"You and I need to go through this," Raymond suggests.

"Yes sir."

"Could we go down to the big house and spread this out?"

"The lady don't want us down there."

"She's still asleep and will be for a while. Carter says she partied quite extensively yesterday. I asked Missus Gilbert to make us some breakfast. She's expecting us."

"The lady ain't gonna like that," Sausalito cautions a second time.

"She'll get over it – that is assuming she ever finds out we were there. Whew, that sure does stink."

"The ground is settlin' some. It's crackin' now that it's dryin' out. I think maybe the vault under the outhouse is leakin'," Sausalito remarks. "It sure does stink worse by the minute."

"I gotta go down and use me the cabana – if you know what I mean," Cincinnati adds with an uncomfortable shift to the side. "And maybe takes me another shower."

"Well, listen to you," Raymond remarks with pleasant surprise. "A shower is a mighty nice thing, isn't it?"

Sausalito frowns at his brother. "He likes the modern conveniences."

"You do too," little brother sasses.

The rooster crows.

Sausalito takes up the tin, then he and Raymond stand. The old man points toward the rusted cook-stove and chuckles. "I was interested to see your *safe* for the paperwork."

"Funny, that's what Mama called it." Sausalito laughs. "She said no thief would think to look in it and it was sure 'nough fire-proof. We ain't cooked on it since we got propane hooked up."

"That's a modern convenience. You don't think propane is *of the Devil* as Carter tells me you like to say?"

"Mama was tired of gettin' ice and startin' fires. She said it was okay to modernize some if it helped day-to-day. Got us a refrigerator and a range."

"I don't blame her there," Raymond agrees, then his face pales. "You have a propane line and a tank? Young man, I know what that smell is. Boys, we gotta get out of here. That smell is leaking propane." The old man grabs his photo album, then corrals the boys and urgently propels them into a run. When they come to the edge of the slog, Raymond pushes them over the edge, then gingerly starts his descent.

BOOM!

The ground beneath them shakes. While they are yet stunned, hunks of pink metal and corrugated steel begin falling from the sky. When they look up, a ball of flame roils at the head of a column of smoke that rises into the deep blue sky.

Chapter Seven

We Got Nothin'

Reverberation from the powerful engines of fire department pumpers pulse throughout the mansion. The driveway is a mass of hoses that lead around the side of the house, then up the slog. Men and women wearing bright green reflective suits bustle about the smoldering remains of the boy's demolished homestead. The grounds of the estate are littered with pink siding and galvanized roofing panels. Countless shards of broken glass lie in the grass and reflect the morning sun. A news helicopter hovering above completes the chaotic scene.

Sausalito and Cincinnati sit together on the patio wrapped in blankets, watching the ordeal with wet eyes above tear-stained cheeks. Further out on the lawn, with mussed hair and wearing bathrobes, Evelyn stands in Carter's embrace with fingers held to her mouth. Floyd is traipsing around the lawn, already pulling the debris into piles. Mrs. Gilbert and Bernard also walk about, gathering broken glass from the grass. Raymond sits at a table near the pool, sorting through the papers from the tin.

"It's too much," Sausalito cries with a breaking heart. "First our home slides off the ridge, then Mama dies, now this. We got nothin' little brother. We got nothin'."

Quietly weeping, Cincinnati says nothing.

"We's goin' back up the hill where we belong. We'll make due."

"What about what Mama did – puttin' us down here an' all?" Cincinnati looks beseechingly at his brother. "You said her spirit done some powerful work."

"I was wrong about that. Mama don't want us down here. I'm thinkin' that it's jus' something that happened. I know where I belong but I know I don't belong here. And the modern propane an' all that *is* of the Devil an' I ain't got no use for none of it. Not no more."

A yellow Porsche Carrera 911 screams up the canyon road and abruptly slows near the mansion's open gates. It turns, carefully maneuvers into the driveway filled with emergency vehicles, then comes to a stop. Cass quickly exits the car, then dashes into the mansion.

Within moments she has careened through the mansion to burst out of the French doors in the back. With wide eyes she looks quickly at Carter and Evelyn, then at the servants cleaning up the lawn, then lastly to the table on the far end of the patio where the boys sit. She runs to them. "Oh my God! Are you okay?" She kneels and runs her hands over their faces. Tears flood her eyes to see that they are fine. Alternately sobbing and laughing, she wipes her eyes and theirs. "I saw this on the news and I was so worried. The whole way here I was praying you boys were all right. Oh, thank God you're okay."

When Carter and Evelyn make their way over to her, Cass rises and goes to Evelyn with a hug. "Oh sweetie, I caught this on the morning report and got here as fast as I could. What can I do?"

While enveloped by Cass's ample arms, Evelyn does her best to shrug.

"Oh, I know you're not a fixer. I'm a fixer. I'll tell you

what I can do." She releases Evelyn, then quickly hugs Carter. "Hey buddy." She looks around. "Is that Raymond? You did get Raymond. Oh good for you. These boys need some help." She raises an arm, waves and shouts, "Yoo hoo, Raymond."

The old man looks up and returns the wave.

Cass's attention goes back to the boys. "I want a hug. I need a hug and you do too. Stand up and get over here." The boys obediently rise as if they were compelled by a force of nature – which they were. Cass suffocates one, then the other into her generous bosom.

She spins to Evelyn. "Have you offered them to stay with you? Of course you haven't. They're staying with you."

"But the..." Evelyn begins to argue, then points toward the child protection workers who are huddled together with the police.

Cass waves her hand. "I'll handle them. Either you take them in or I'll take them home with me..." She rolls her eyes upward in thought, then shakes her head. "...which they'd hate because I live in a high-rise. So, they're staying with you and I don't want to hear any of your crap about it."

"Listen boys." She turns to the boys. "I kind of swoop in like the Tasmanian Devil which I'm pretty sure you don't know what that is, but anyway, that's because that's how I am. I run my own business so I gotta fly 'cause I'm already late and I have a million things to do today. Evelyn and Carter are going to set you up with rooms to stay in. I'll come back this evening and we're going shopping for clothing and whatever else you need. I know you're broken-hearted what with your mother passing and your place ending up down here and now all this. I can't tell you how bad I feel for you.

86

"It's going to get better and we're going to make it get better. What beautiful boys you both are. I'll be back and don't put up with any of her," she points at her closest friend, "crap." She spontaneously grabs, then hugs both of the boys once more. Then turning to Evelyn, she actually looks at her for a moment. "You look like shit." Cass waves her hand up and down Evelyn's disheveled appearance. "You should do something about that." She quickly waves at Carter, then blows a kiss to Raymond. As she struts toward the child protection workers, she starts waving both arms. "We have this handled..." she begins.

The boys and the wealthy couple look at one another just a bit stunned from the F-5 tornado that hadn't been forecast, but just blew through, a.k.a. Cass.

"Pizza?" Cincinnati asks.

"Sandwich," Mrs. Gilbert replies.

"Left over pizza?" Cincinnati counters.

"Sandwich," Mrs. Gilbert replies.

"Frozen pizza?"

"Sandwich."

An ingratiating toothy smile.

A humorless glower.

"Okay. Sandwich." Cincinnati complies.

"I don't negotiate," Mrs. Gilbert informs the lad. In her hand is a gourmet sandwich on a plate that she plunks down on the breakfast nook table in front of the boy. "If someone ever took you hostage and I had to pay the ransom, you'd be dead. Just so ya know." When Cincinnati starts to lift the bread to see what's inside Mrs. Gilbert warns, "Don't you do it. You will eat what I give you to eat and I don't want to hear no fussing."

Cincinnati looks at her uncertainly, then lowers the bread and picks the sandwich up to take a bite.

"There's yer chips." She pushes a large bowl of chips toward him. "And yer soda." A glass filled with ice and a can of soda is also shoved in front of him. "Eat up." Mrs. Gilbert walks across the expanse of kitchen where she stops to look out the French doors. Sausalito is now walking atop the mound, picking at the burnt wreckage. "Yer brother gonna eat?" she asks.

"Doubt it," the boy replies while sneaking a look inside his sandwich.

Evelyn enters the kitchen now dressed and nicely coifed. With jet-black contacts lens in her eyes, she immediately makes the observation of Cincinnati (filthy hillbilly #2) sitting in the nook. Her semi-polite smile looks as painful as it most likely is. Mrs. Gilbert turns toward her. "Comin' right up." The housekeeper plows over to the fridge to retrieve a beautiful green salad and vitamin water, then heads toward the table in the nook.

Evelyn not so discreetly clears her throat. "I thought I might sit by the pool."

"Very well," Mrs. Gilbert concedes, then nods her head toward Cincinnati as she changes direction. "Come on, kid. Yer eatin' by the pool."

When Evelyn whines like a sad puppy, Mrs. Gilbert stops and rolls her eyes. "What?"

With a subtle shift of her head toward the boy who is gathering up his meal, Evelyn's nostrils flare and her eyebrows rise.

"Listen, Missy. I ain't puttin' up with yer crap today. Either yer both eatin' at the pool or yer both eatin' in here. What's it gonna be?"

Moments later, both Evelyn and Cincinnati are seated under the shade of an umbrella at a table near the pool. The boy watches Evelyn's every move in between ripping savage bites from his sandwich and chewing them with his mouth more open than closed. Evelyn eats meagerly, trying to only look at the salad on her fork or the nearby nude statue.

"You are so pretty," Cincinnati comments dreamily between savage bites.

With an uncertain smile accompanied by a brief glance his way, Evelyn nods. "Thank you."

"I'm gonna draw me a picture of you." Cincinnati's eyes subtly dart over to the statue.

"That's nice," Evelyn curtly replies – not quite understanding the implication of the proposed drawing.

Cincinnati smiles gregariously.

Evelyn blanches at his teeth that are loaded with food and now exposed by a smile that will not depart from the boy's face no matter how badly she wishes it would.

"Could I try me one a' those?" The boy points at a slice of sweet pepper on the salad. After a slight shudder, Evelyn begins to daintily pluck it from the salad with her fork. The boy's fingers preempt her effort. "That's okay, I gots it." He grabs it along with a few other ingredients – which he tosses back. He pops the pepper into his mouth. "*Ummm.* That is good. It looked good and it is."

After looking with despair at her contaminated salad, Evelyn discreetly pushes it aside.

"You ain't gonna eat that?"

Another disdainful shudder is accompanied with a microscopic shake of Evelyn's head.

"Hey Sausalito," the boy suddenly yells in a volume that could be heard across the neighborhood. "You want a salad? The lady ain't gonna finish hers." Bits of chewed sandwich pepper the entire table as well as Evelyn's hands, arms, and glass of water. She begins to gag. As Sausalito starts to descend the slog, Cincinnati notices the mess he made. "Oh, sorry." He takes a napkin, then begins to brush splattered food off Evelyn's arm. "Mama always said that eatin' with me was like eatin' with one a' them sprinklers that goes; chi, chi, chi." More food is sprayed on the table from his sprinkler imitation.

Evelyn's gag becomes a convulsion.

"You okay?" the boy asks innocently.

Evelyn rises and rushes from the table without an explanation.

As Evelyn runs into the house, Sausalito meanders toward the table by the pool. "What's with her?" he asks.

"Don't know." Cincinnati shrugs. "Maybe she gots to go to the bathroom. Try these. These is good." He picks up another pepper and then pushes the salad toward his despondent brother. "You ain't ate nothin' all day."

"Ain't much in the mood." Sausalito picks at the salad. "We got nothin', little brother."

"Got each other. We ain't dead. We was as close to bein' dead as we're likely ever to be a couple times now and we ain't yet. I think Mama's lookin' out for us."

Sausalito shakes his head while eating a couple of the greens.

"I seen my room," Cincinnati informs his brother. "Missus Gilbert showed it to me. It's the fanciest damn thing you ever saw. She said you ought ta be the first to see yers so she wouldn't show me."

Big brother looks at his younger brother's happy face and shakes his head. "Don't guess you rightly understand all that's goin' on. You think this is some kind 'a adventure. It ain't. This is the end of ever' thin' we had. Ever'way we was."

Mrs. Gilbert steps out from the French doors headed their direction. They watch her approach. As she nears the table, she extends a cordless phone to Sausalito. "Mister Bartel would like to speak with you."

Sausalito looks cluelessly at the telephone, then stands and heads toward the doors.

"Where are you going?" Mrs. Gilbert shakes the receiver. He looks at it. She rolls her eyes and releases an annoyed breath. "You ain't never seen a phone?"

He looks at the device in her hand.

"Oh, dear Lord." She pushes a button, then holds it up to his head. "Put this part on your ear, then just talk like normal."

He holds the phone up to his ear. "What should I say?"

"Ya say, hello."

"Hello?"

Apparently, Raymond begins to speak because the young man suddenly jerks the phone away and stares at it with wide and surprised eyes.

"He' ain't in it." Mrs. Gilbert pushes the receiver back toward his head. "Good Lord, you boy's ain't from this century."

With wide eyes moving side to side, Sausalito listens intently. "Okay. - I understand. - I understand." He nods. He nods some more.

"Ya have to talk. He can't see ya nodding." Mrs. Gilbert's holds her hands threateningly toward Sausalito's throat like she wants to strangle the boy.

"Uh huh. - Yes. - Uh huh. - Okay." Sausalito's eyes squint. He looks at the phone which now emits a dial-tone, then at Mrs. Gilbert. "It's makin' a noise."

"That means you're done. Did he say goodbye?"

Sausalito nods, then replies, "Yes."

"I can see you. When he says bye, you say bye, and then you push this button right here." Mrs. Gilbert demonstrates.

The young man looks at her full face, then over at his

brother, whose jaw has dropped at the wonder of it all. Sausalito looks at the phone. "Where is Mister Bartel?"

"He's downtown in his office."

"Of the Devil."

Sausalito holds on for dear life as Cass careens her yellow Carrera along a busy boulevard. Since the top is down, the wind rushes around the windshield and blows the boys' hair into their faces. "Are you sure I can't talk you into haircuts?" Cass yells over the wind and engine.

Sausalito, griping the armrest with both hands, shakes his head as Cass gleefully negotiates a corner at top speed.

"Well, too bad. You'd be even more gorgeous than you are now," she replies at the top of her lungs.

"Are we goin' to the Walmarts?" Cincinnati shouts from the back seat.

"We don't do Walmart," Cass yells back. "It's not a "the" and it isn't a plural but it is a frightening place filled with frightening people. When your oil change is done, they page your name over one-hundred thousand garishly lit square feet of linoleum tile. We're going to a clothier. I was thinking Neiman Marcus, Nordstrom's or Bloomingdale's."

"Do they have tee shirts with cartoon characters on 'em? I was thinkin' one or two of them and a pair a new boots," Cincinnati replies. After quiver of loathing, Cass flips on the turn signal and changes direction.

Later, inside a mall department store, Cass watches Cincinnati who is happily sorting through a table of cartoon tees. Sausalito, who is not fully embracing the shopping experience, peers curiously at a series of monotone gray mannequins without faces. Bundled in Cass's arms are several pairs of little boy jeans and shirts. "I'm carrying clothing. I'm actually carrying clothing," Cass laments. She looks around again for the elusive department store sales clerk that is said to exist – but could be one of those darn urban legends. "Is there no help? Is there no Cappuccino? No Latté? Where are the pastries? How do people shop like this?"

"I was me in a Walmarts once," Cincinnati idly comments as he holds up a tee. "It was amazing. I never seen anything like it an' they had ever' thing you could think a'. Mama said there was some things you jus' had to buy at a store like that an' so that day she needed me and Sausalito to help carry it on the bus home so we got to go."

"I think we should work us on some sentence structure and grammar, but that aside, I suppose if it was a life and death situation, I could go in one." Cass rolls her eyes to imagine that particular scenario, but then quivers. "It's a place where tattooed women and street urchins find others of their kind to procreate with. They actually page parents when they find their snotty-nosed toddlers wandering around." She shudders. "Can you imagine? It's nothing but pierced lips, saggy drawers, halter-tops and scooters driven by enormous people with skin growths."

"Someday, I'm gonna go me in one again," Cincinnati says as he lays another selection over Cass's arm. "I gots me one for ever' day ah the week now. What's next?"

Having moved on from the mannequins, Sausalito has taken to observing other young people who are idly poking through clothes they have no intention of buying. He observes their trendy, if not edgy, style of dress with his head slightly tilted to one side. "Honey?" Cass interrupts. "Do you have everything you want here?"

He nods.

"Shoes will be next," Cass declares. "I guess I'm expected to go lay these on a counter somewhere. Where is the help? Honestly, this isn't shopping. This is gathering or hunting or some other barbaric experience."

"You complain a lot," Cincinnati informs her.

"I'm rich. That's what we do."

The boys' arms are loaded with sacks as Cass, with a huge, bedazzled purse in one hand and car keys in the other, struts across the mall parking lot ahead of them. She has left her Carrera parked diagonally across four entire parking places on the periphery of the lot. The lights flash and horn beeps as she presses the remote. Then the top rises and begins to fold. Sausalito stops dead in his tracks. "Lookit what yer car is doin'."

Cass dangles the keys. "I did that."

"This is one crazy world."

The trunk pops open – again without them anywhere near. The eyes of both boys grow wide. "Put what you can in the trunk, then we'll cram the rest in the back seat."

"I'm surprised it doesn't start itself," Sausalito sarcastically comments.

Cass pushes another button. While they're still several feet away, the car starts. She smiles at the boys' dropped jaws. "You never said what you thought of the car…"

"It's real nice," Sausalito answers while he and his brother begin to pack their purchases into the trunk.

"*Nice?* It's a kick-in-the-ass." Cass throws her head back ecstatically. "I love this car! You cannot believe how much fun it is to drive this machine."

"Mama said driving is of the Devil," Cincinnati casually informs her.

"Your mama never drove a Porsche Carrera nine-eleven." Cass winks, smiles broadly, then plops into the driver's seat.

A pickup drives past. "Learn how to park," the driver yells from his window.

"Kiss my well-rounded ass," Cass yells back.

Dinner plates have been nearly cleaned in the elegant dining room of the mansion. Carter and Evelyn occupy the ends of the twelve-foot-long table. The boys and Raymond are seated near Carter while Cass sits near Evelyn, who still averts her gaze from *The Sprinkler*, as she not-that-affectionately now refers to Cincinnati.

Raymond's very expensive suit coat is draped over the back of his chair. His impeccably pressed white shirt and bold silk tie nearly sparkle under the chandelier's lights. He leans forward on his forearms to speak to Sausalito. "Without a home on the land, I have no precedent to prevent the landslide from being trucked away."

With his eyes downcast, Sausalito nods.

"I'm working on how we could possibly rectify your mother's estate without a certificate of death. As of right now, no one knows about her passing so we have some time. Carter tells me the authorities are pressuring him to get the earth removed as soon as possible. There are underground utilities that can rupture from its weight. You understand the urgency, right?"

"Yes sir."

"I have a landscaper scheduled to come tomorrow," Carter interjects. "He'll make sure the area where your mother is buried remains untouched. I've instructed him to make a small knoll there. He doesn't know why, other than I want a knoll there."

Sausalito nods. "So tomorrow? The tractors an' trucks come tomorrow?"

"Yes." Raymond nods. "I understand you'd like to go back up top on the ridge. All the land in this area is owned by a very powerful corporation. I rather doubt they'd let you squat up there and even if you could, the authorities won't let anyone build any structure up there until the ground is stabilized. The corporation is apparently responsible for re-stabilizing the hillside, so there are going to be engineers crawling all over the canyon and ridge over the next few weeks. Between the two incidents, this affair really got the government's attention. Until something else comes along, they're going to be like a dog with a bone; they aren't letting go of this. You don't want to be between the government and a corporation. You need to come to grips that you'll be staying with the Chatsblythes for the foreseeable future."

Sausalito turns toward the far end of the table where Evelyn has been hanging on Raymond's every word. "I know you don't want us here," Sausalito begins. "We'll be goin' as soon as we can."

"Don't be ridiculous." Cass intercepts the conversation. "I've convinced the authorities that you've always shared the same address and that they don't have the right to say anything's changed. Then to be safe, I told 'em that our gorgeous little hunk of man, Sausalito here, is at least eighteen – if not twenty-one. Human Services is pretty confused right now and people like us with lawyers and money scare the crap out of them. The Chatsblythes have assured me that you're welcome here as long as you want or need to be here. Isn't that right, Evelyn?"

Evelyn releases a pained breath and smiles sickly.

With morning light beginning to illuminate Sausalito's new bedroom, the two boys lay buried in soft covers together in the same bed. While Cincinnati snores away, Sausalito stares at the ceiling with dark rings around his bloodshot eyes. The room is a tastefully decorated suite furnished with modern woods and painted in hues of green and cranberry. It is as foreign as it could possibly be from anything either boy has ever known.

The dull vibration of trucks and heavy equipment in motion begins to permeate the mansion. Piercing back-up beepers add to the symphony. Cincinnati's snoring begins to break up with a collection of moans and whimpers. Gradually, he begins to stretch and squirm beneath the covers. At a point, he rises up on his elbows, then yawns as he looks around.

"That was amazing. I know what sleepin' in Heaven feels like." He rubs the sleep from his eyes while observing his brother's tormented stare at the ceiling. "You didn't sleep so good, huh?"

"Didn't sleep at all," Sausalito replies hoarsely.

Listening to the noises, the boy asks, "Is that the tractors?"

"That's them."

"Well, I wanna watch."

"Jus' another adventure for you," Sausalito grouses.

"Yer jus' sour on ever' thing right now. You need to get over stuff. Ain't nothin' you can do but let it go."

Sausalito grunts. "I can't do this."

"Why not? We never had it so good."

"Ain't right. Ain't us." Sausalito massages his face with his hands. "Think I'm gonna go find the pack – do me some huntin' – get back to my roots. You can stay here with these rich folks. You like all this fanciness and the cars and the shoppin'. You have yer adventure an' I'll have mine."

As he's looking at his big brother's emotionless stare, Cincinnati's brow creases. "So, that's it? Yer goin'?"

"For a while." Sausalito shrugs. "I'll be back sometime."

"Think the pack will let you come back? You're pretty big now."

"Long as I ain't a challenge, it should be okay."

Still staring at the side of his big brother's face, Cincinnati asks, "How am I gonna sleep tonight with you gone an' all? I was scared to death a that big ol' room all by myself. That's why I came in here."

"It ain't all about you, Cincinnati."

"Ain't all about you either, Sausalito."

"Bernard," Evelyn snaps into the phone. "Bernard. Are you there?"

Mrs. Gilbert's eyes shift from the breakfast she's preparing over to where Evelyn, wearing a robe, is grousing into the telephone.

"I know it's seven o'clock. I have got to get out of here. Those machines are already driving me insane. I cannot believe they thought it was okay to start on that mess at this hour. Imbeciles!" As Evelyn wanders around with the cordless phone, she catches the reflection of her wild hair and puffy face in a mirror. She mashes one side of her hair to at least make the mess symmetrical. She continues to grouse. "Apparently Mister Chatsblythe neglected to inform Cretin Earth Removal Bastards Incorporated that I sleep until nine. I need the car brought around. I called the spa and told them it was an emergency." Evelyn places a fingertip gingerly on the rim of a puffy bag beneath her eye.

She sneers at the phone and Bernard's obviously unsympathetic response. Evelyn shakes her head and rolls her eyes as she listens. "You don't need to be dressed. You're driving the car. No one is going to see you. Do you think I'm getting dressed? I look a wreck but I have got to get out of here. I can't even think to select clothing. I'll order something while I'm soaking in the mud-bath. Chop, chop, Bernard. I need the car." Evelyn hangs up, then looks over at Mrs. Gilbert's disapproving frown.

"Oh stuff it," Evelyn sasses. "He's my driver and I hardly ever ask for something like this. Oh, confound the racket! Do none of them ever drive forward? If Bernard isn't out front in two minutes, I'm going to go out there and disconnect those blasted beepers myself."

After rudely placing the phone on the unit, Evelyn meanders deeper into the kitchen. With her nose wrinkled, she looks into the frying pan Mrs. Gilbert is tending to. "It's for the boys," Mrs. Gilbert answers the unasked question. "Breakfast burritos."

With a raise of her eyebrows, Evelyn puckers her lips, then sucks them in.

"It ain't for you 'cause it's real food."

"It's a heart-attack on a tortilla." Evelyn sniffs.

"I'll eat two," Mrs. Gilbert offers. "Maybe then I won't have to listen to your bitching."

"If I'm ever able to fire the help, you better pack your bags, old woman."

"If you're ever able to fire the help, I'll quit."

"Whatever. I can't imagine what you're going to do with those boys all day, but good luck to you. I imagine it'll be a regular Hillbilly-Pa-Losa. I suspect you all, or y'all, as you people would say, will have built a still in the backyard by the time I return."

"In a perfect world, there would already be one there."

"Whatever. I couldn't possibly hear if the limousine is ready over all this commotion. Y'all have a hootenanny of a day." With another disdainful sneer at the pan of burrito fixin's, Evelyn turns and prepares to sail from the kitchen like the overly dramatic actress she might have been. The boys enter. Mildly startled, but mostly dismayed, Evelyn tightens her robe and forces a courteous, but brief smile.

Cincinnati wears a colorful cartoon tee and crisp jean

shorts – both with sharp creases and bearing price tags from the store. Sausalito wears only the jeans and boots he escaped from the trailer with and a tee shirt. Evelyn looks up and down both of them while holding her breath.

"Good morning," Mrs. Gilbert calls over he shoulder with an unusual degree of cheerfulness – mostly to annoy the mistress.

"Mornin'," Cincinnati mumbles.

Sausalito says nothing.

Noticing the drawn expressions on both boys' faces, but not caring enough to ask, Evelyn starts to edge past, but then curiously lingers with a slight crease of possible concern forming in her brow.

"I guess this is actually not a happy day for you boys," Mrs. Gilbert concedes.

"Not so much," Cincinnati confirms, then looks at his brother sadly.

"Well, you boys have a seat. Breakfast is comin' right up."

"Could you wrap mine up?" Sausalito asks.

"Yeah, and give him mine. I ain't so hungry," Cincinnati adds.

"Now boys, I suppose I ought to explain something to you since you're living here. I pretty much run this kitchen. Both of you sit yer little butts down right over there. I ain't wrappin' anything to go. When it's time to eat, ya eat and that's all there is to it. Now…"

"He's leavin'," Cincinnati interrupts dejectedly.

With no ceremony or goodbye, Sausalito walks past everyone toward the French doors. He opens one, then steps out. As he starts to walk toward the hillside, Mrs. Gilbert turns back toward Cincinnati.

The boy shrugs weakly, looking as if he's about to cry. "He's gonna go back to the pack. Says he can't live like this."

The housekeeper hastily grabs a hunk of foil, flings a couple burritos into it, then rushes out the door. Through the glass, Evelyn and Cincinnati watch her run up to Sausalito. They speak a moment. While he stands rigidly, she wraps her arms around him in a hug. The teen goes on his way while Mrs. Gilbert returns to the house wiping her eyes.

Evelyn blinks a couple times before the horn of the limousine blares from somewhere outside. She looks at Cincinnati, starts to extend a hand toward his shoulder, then withdraws it and silently steps away.

Chapter Eight

I Was Wrong

Evelyn reclines in the warm embrace of a vat of black mud. It bubbles and roils as hints of steam rise from the muck. Covering her face is a green masque with cucumber slices positioned over her eyes. Soft music plays on strategically positioned speakers. All around her are burning candles and aromatic oils simmering in pots.

Instead of relaxed, deep, rhythmic breathing, her breaths are shallow and short. The green masque has begun to crumble around her mouth as she seems unable to either smile or frown or settle on anything in between. "Damnit," she finally exclaims and raises a hand from the muck to pull the ring that summons the attendant. She raises her head and takes the cucumber slices from her eyes just as a door opens behind her. A young woman attendant enters. Evelyn turns to face her and bluntly states, "I have to go."

Cincinnati sits at a table near the pool, watching as the mound that had been his home disappears. Front-end loaders make quick work of the earth, rapidly removing large swaths which are promptly dumped into a waiting queue of large trucks. The roar of numerous diesel engines is nearly deafening. The outhouse and remains of the trailer and the rusted junk are gone. The landscaper and his crew have already begun to shore the banks of the unmarked burial site with stone. A load of top-soil and a flatbed of sod wait in the street. By evening, no one will suspect anything had ever happened at 1219 Happy Canyon Drive.

With her cranium wrapped in a stylish scarf and no make-up whatsoever on her face, Evelyn pokes her head out the French doors. Wearing attire that looks something like a moo-moo, she walks over to the poolside. Cincinnati attempts an unconvincing smile by raising one corner of his mouth. Evelyn looks between him and the disappearing homestead. When the boy doesn't even attempt another smile, Evelyn begins to place her hand on his, but withdraws it. "I know today has got to be very difficult for you. What do you say we get out of here for a little while?" she asks sympathetically.

The limousine is parked across the street from a mom and pop ice cream shop on a shady lane. Evelyn and Cincinnati sit at a table beneath an umbrella. While the boy gregariously licks a swirl of ice cream from a mounded cone, Evelyn watches disdainfully with napkins at-the-ready should *The Sprinkler* suddenly activate. "You want a lick?" Cincinnati extends the cone toward her.

After observing a glisten of spit that shines in the daylight, Evelyn responds coldly. "No. Thank you."

"Back in the days when Mama still felt good she took me to get this here ice creams a couple times. It's real good."

"I'm sure it is."

"How come you didn't get one?"

With a slight roll of her eyes, Evelyn explains, "I have to watch my weight."

"Yer skinny as a rail, Mama would say. Why you got to

watch your weight?"

"I am a certain size. I need to remain a certain size."

"Cass and Missus Gilbert don't watch what they eat and they're plenty big."

"Both of those facts have occurred to me. Is there a reason why you simply cannot either eat or speak? Why must you eat *and* speak?"

The boy shrugs.

"I would do a lot better around you if you did one or the other."

While smilin at the comment, Cincinnati licks more ice cream. "You don't like the sprinkler?" He draws a breath in preparation to imitate the action.

"*Don't do it*. Absolutely *never* do that again," Evelyn snaps.

The boy puckers up.

"Sorry. It's just that I don't want to vomit just now. If we, and by we, I mean you, could just eat the ice cream with no sprinkler and no flying debris I would be eternally grateful."

While Cincinnati silently resumes licking the cone, Evelyn peers curiously around them. Common people are everywhere on this summer afternoon: strolling, walking dogs, running, biking, snacking. The banality of it all is simply staggering. That they believe they are happy is unfathomable – yet they seem to be.

"How come Bernard doesn't want ice cream?" Cincinnati asks.

"Bernard is a driver. He drives. He does not accompany us on outings."

"He probably wants some and he's right over there."

"Then he can come here on his day off. I thought we were going to work on eating the ice cream and not speaking."

"I get ideas."

"Obviously. Could you put them on hold?"

"I could try."

"That would be stupendous."

Cincinnati silently licks more ice cream while Evelyn observes his mussed hair. When she notices the white crust of dried tears beneath his eyes and their tracks down his cheeks, a slight, sad smile begins to emerge on her face. "You're a happy child. This week you've lost your home and everything but the pants you were wearing and the boots on your feet. Your mother died and your bother's left you – yet you're happy to sit here and lick a two-dollar ice cream cone. Your only concern in the world right now is that Bernard doesn't have ice cream."

Cincinnati smiles his goofy smile.

After puckering her lips and tapping the table in contemplation, Evelyn smiles slightly and rises. "I'll be right back." She crosses the street and heads toward the limousine. After leaning down to speak into the driver's window for a moment, she steps back. Bernard gets out, then walks back across the street with her. After a couple minutes at the window of the stand, Evelyn turns away with a baby cone in her hand. Bernard has obviously ordered a double.

As they approach the table, Cincinnati smiles with ice cream all over his teeth.

Raymond has once again joined the Chatsblythes for dinner. They all sit at a table near the pool as the sun draws close to the western ridge. The noise and trucks are long gone. The landslide has been replaced with a flat expanse of newly-laid lawn. Loretta's burial knoll stands just to the other side of the fountain, partially shored to stabilize its transformation. Pallets of materials, piles of stone, as well as the landscaper's idle equipment sit nearby with intentions of completing the transformation the following day. Cincinnati mostly looks between the void that had been his home, the grave knoll of his mother, and the dinner he's not eating.

"Your brother picked a very inopportune time to go run with the pack," Raymond comments casually between bites.

Cincinnati looks at him and squints his eyes questioningly.

"His leaving today was not the best timing," Raymond clarifies.

"I know. I miss him."

"I'm sorry. I guess I'm focused on the legal and paperwork aspects. Of course you miss him," Raymond apologizes. "You must feel very lonely."

The boy nods.

"Do you think if we hiked up the hill this evening, we could find him?" Carter asks.

Cincinnati shakes his head. "He don't want to be found. He'll come back when he's ready."

"Tomorrow we really need to work out some sort of guardianship." Raymond raises his eyebrows at Carter and Evelyn. "Loretta's education plans and records were kept in the trailer, so they were all destroyed. We have to make decisions about school. We have a lot to do. What we don't want is Protective Services further disrupting these boys' world if there is any hope for them to have something familiar in their lives."

Raymond takes a bite then addresses Cincinnati again. "Your mother left explicit instructions. She apparently knew she was dying so she did a few things to make the transition easier. There is a lot of notarized paperwork already filled out with her signature on it. Some of it isn't quite kosher, so I can't be a party to it. But someone without my knowledge could fill in the blanks in good conscience and have a legally-binding document."

Cincinnati looks at Raymond blankly.

"Your mother made things easier than I was expecting them to be."

"Oh."

Raymond faces Carter and Evelyn, then continues. "The guardianship papers just need a name and address filled in. They're also signed and pre-notarized."

Both look back at him about as blankly.

"Anyway," Raymond shifts in his chair, "most of her instructions refer to her friend at the bank. Unfortunately that is a closed door because I can't get any information without having Sausalito with me. His name is on the account." Raymond comments to Cincinnati, "It's highly unusual that your mother trusted a bank."

"Mama liked this lady at the bank real good. Missus Conley. Said we could trust her," Cincinnati responds. "Why is that a-usual?" he asks.

"To most people with beliefs like your mother's, banks aren't that much different from the government, which she believed to be – pardon the expression – of the Devil. Mistrust of government and banks kind of go hand-in-hand."

"Mama said we'd shoot ourselves in the foot if we didn't have the bank."

"Your mama was a smart lady. She must have had her reasons." Raymond picks up his napkin and wipes his mouth. "Carter, Evelyn, it's been a pleasure. Cincinnati, there isn't much more I can do until your brother comes back. You let me know when that happens. Feel free to give me a call with any concerns. Everyone here knows how to reach me day or night." He pushes his chair back, stands, then turns to Carter and Evelyn. "Thank you for a lovely dinner. I'll thank Missus Gilbert on my way out." He pushes the chair back in. "I left those guardianship papers on the credenza just inside the entry if anyone is curious to have a look at them."

This time the blank looks come from all the faces at the table.

"Did I mention how wonderful and natural it felt to sit down with all of you for dinner tonight? *Together*," Raymond emphasizes. "*Here*." He smiles. "Think about it." He smiles, winks, then walks away.

Carter and Evelyn exchange an uncomfortable, if not mortified glance, then turn. Cincinnati quickly looks down and resumes picking at his food with even less interest than before. Kids know when they are not wanted.

The limousine, with all its doors open, is parked in the driveway in the cool of late day shadows cast by the setting sun. The stereo plays lowly while Bernard lovingly uses a soft cloth to polish every surface. He sings along contentedly as he works. Cincinnati watches him from the front steps, then after a while, wanders over. Bernard looks up at the boy's approach. "What are you up to?"

Cincinnati shrugs. "Not much. What are you doin'?"

"Missus Chatsblythe doesn't like fingerprints or dust inside the car so I keep it spotless for her." Bernard thinks a moment. "Never knew she appreciated that or anything else I did until today."

Cincinnati nods. "Can I help?"

"Let me see your hands."

Cincinnati holds them out.

"No," Bernard responds flatly as he continues his task. "You can watch."

"I helped Floyd today."

"Floyd works with dirt. One might say you are a natural to help Floyd."

"Floyd said that too. He said I was a good helper. An' you know what else?"

"I'm sure I don't."

"The goats and chickens that wasn't killed in the 'splosion, done run off. Floyd said no offense, but he was glad 'a that. Don't you do nothing for fun?"

"This is fun. I bet you haven't seen the other cars. Go wash your hands and I'll show you how I spend my time. You like cars, right?"

"Don't know. Only seen 'em from a distance. Rode in a bus a few times but only two cars now; Cass's an' this. This one sure is big an' nice and quiet."

"It's very nice. I don't suppose you know what a Bentley is."

Cincinnati shakes his head.

"Go wash your hands real good front and back and all the way up to your elbow and I'll show you. And blow your nose and go to the bathroom. I want all your bodily processes done before you get inside an automobile like the one I'm going to show you. Just to let you know, I better not find a booger or a slobber anywhere on or in it."

Carter and Evelyn stroll hand-in-hand down the canyon drive as the evening's shadows lengthen all around them. "Given the tragedies those boys have suffered," Carter begins, "I know I shouldn't be as happy and relieved as I was tonight to see the place looking nearly normal."

Evelyn's smile holds a hint of distraction. "Yes. It is a relief."

"Did the landscaper show you the plans for Loretta's knoll? I actually think it will add to the grounds."

"He offered. I just wasn't in the right frame of mind."

Evelyn attempts another smile, then continues to look forlornly ahead.

"What's wrong, Evelyn?"

"That boy. That poor, lonely boy."

"I thought you were officially calling him the *Savage Little Heathen* or *The Sprinkler* these days."

Evelyn shrugs. "He's so broken-hearted. It just kills me to look at him, or even think of the magnitude of his losses."

"Well, you know what Raymond was hinting at with all that guardianship talk, don't you?"

"He wasn't very discreet."

"He wasn't trying to be."

Evelyn snorts, then offers a bemused, "Huh."

Carter repeats questioningly, "Huh?"

Evelyn shrugs. "I was watching Cincinnati help Floyd earlier. The old fool and the filthy midget were digging a hole together – it was kind of cute. Then a half hour ago when Cincinnati and Bernard took off down the street in the Bentley, I wanted to take a picture. Bernard was laughing. In five years I've never seen Bernard laugh. *Ever.* I don't think I've ever even seen him smile."

"You don't think they were stealing it, do you?" Carter asks with mock alarm.

Evelyn laughs. "I suspect they will eventually bring it back."

"After they drag race and burn donuts with it."

"You can't burn donuts in an all-wheel-drive," Evelyn retorts, then gently shoves Carter sideways.

"Whatever." Carter playfully shoves her back, then stops walking. "I heard a rumor today. Missus Gilbert told me that you took Cincinnati and Bernard for ice cream. She was very proud of you for doing that. She didn't think you, '*had it in ya*.'"

Evelyn looks down. A demure smile creeps across her face. "I kind of enjoyed it."

Carter admires her thoughtful, downturned eyes and the curve of her lips. "I glanced at those guardianship papers while I was waiting for you to put your shoes on," he confesses.

"I looked at them when I asked you to go get your phone," Evelyn admits.

They laugh, clasp hands, then continue their walk.

The late-night news anchors have barely started their goodnights when Carter raises the remote around Evelyn's head and sends them on their way. She snuggles deeper into his arms for a moment. He kisses the top of her head. At the other end of the great-room sofa, Cincinnati sits bolt upright, staring at the television's blank screen. His face is pale when he asks, "All that's goin' on in the world?"

"All that and more," Carter assures. "Not too much of it good."

"Of the Devil."

"That's one I'll agree with you on." Carter stretches. "Let's get you into bed."

The boy turns toward him with a look that is nothing less than mortified.

"I heard from Missus Gilbert that you slept in your brother's room last night." Carter stands. "We can leave a light on for you if you'd like. You'll eventually get used to having your own bedroom." Carter opens his arm toward Cincinnati.

Although the boy's expression doesn't change, Cincinnati obediently rises. As he is about to step into Carter's open arm, Evelyn awkwardly raises her hand to touch his shoulder. She adds, "You'll get used to it,

111

goodnight." She lowers her hand before it ever makes it to his shoulder, then smiles briefly.

The smile Cincinnati returns is just as brief.

Nine o'clock dawns bright, if not early. Wearing a fluffy robe and with her hair in a frazzle, Evelyn staggers into the kitchen in mid-yawn. The crew working on the knoll has obviously been informed about making noise, as all the equipment instantly fires up at the top of the hour. The sudden commotion prompts an immediate shudder from the drowsy mistress. "Cretins," she utters under her breath.

At the sink stands Mrs. Gilbert half-heartedly rinsing a few dishes. She looks every bit as enthusiastic as Evelyn when she glances her direction. She releases a weary sigh, turns off the water, dries her hands, and walks to the refrigerator in a slouch. She opens the door, takes out a yogurt, walks to the table, sets it down, pulls a spoon from the pocket of her apron, drops it next to the yogurt, then plops down in a chair across from the yogurt. "Eat up," she suggests miserably, then folds her arms and lays her head down on top of them.

After observing her a moment, Evelyn asks, "What happened to presentation?"

"Ta da," Mrs. Gilbert replies from beneath her folded arms.

"Are you ill?"

"Only in the heart."

Evelyn hesitantly makes her way over to the table, pulls out her chair and sits quietly. "I can smell the stench of your heart attack special. I was expecting the gawdawful sight of a whole platter of them."

The housekeeper's head remains on her arms.

"So, no morning surliness?" Evelyn questions in disbelief. "No tit-for-tat? No battle royal?"

The housekeeper says nothing.

As she pulls the foil back on the plastic container, Evelyn observes the housekeeper with a crease of concern forming between her eyebrows. "Are you sure you're all right?"

"He's gone," Mrs. Gilbert finally explains, still speaking into her arms.

"Well, that was yesterday," Evelyn quips with an abrupt wave of her hand. "Like you always tell me, *get over it*. Cincinnati says he'll be back eventually."

"Not him. The other one. Our little boy's gone too," Mrs. Gilbert moans.

"Cincinnati?"

"Went to his room. Bed ain't been touched. All the clothes Cass bought him are gone. One of the French doors was unlocked this morning. He up and left. They're both gone now."

"*Noooooooo!*" Evelyn slumps. "*Noooooooo,*" she repeats as she leans forward on her elbows looking as if she's about to cry. "*Noooooooooo.*" She extends a hand to touch the housekeeper's arm, but pulls it back. "Cincinnati's gone? That just sucks." She looks around the kitchen with a heart both hurt and sad. "I was up half the night wondering if I should sign that guardianship paperwork. *Noooooo*. Well, if this doesn't beat all. We opened our home and neither one wanted it. Who wouldn't want this home?" She sighs. She sighs again. "I know you liked having him around. I'm sorry, Missus Gilbert."

Mrs. Gilbert finally lifts her head from her arms and sits upright. "Thanks Missy. I was so proud of you yesterday for taking him for ice cream. I had all these thoughts of us having a whole family here. I stayed up last night goin' through my recipes for the most grease-laden, artery-clogging concoctions I could make. I was hoping to gag you every time you walked in the kitchen."

Evelyn swoons. "Oh, that is so sweet."

"Don't mention it. I was gonna blossom you up to a size twelve."

"*Ohhhhhh.*" Evelyn beams. "You do love me."

The muffled racket of the landscaper's roaring, beeping equipment suddenly rushes in from outside and fills the house. The women turn toward the French doors. Cincinnati enters, then turns and pushes the door closed behind him. When the noise is once again muffled, he exclaims, "I was sound asleep and dreamin' an' all a sudden there was all this noise and I swear the whole damn ground started shakin'!"

The women blink.

"Are we havin' those burritos again? I likes me those burritos."

The women blink again.

Summoning a roar of her own, Mrs. Gilbert barks, "Where have you been?"

The boy points toward the doors. "Outside."

"*You slept outside?*"

Cincinnati rubs sleep from his eyes as he nods. "I slept next to Mama." He lifts up his Spiderman T-shirt to reveal the layers of clothing that cover his tummy. "I knew you wouldn't a wanted me dirtying up a blanket, so I put on all my clothes to keep warm."

Mrs. Gilbert bites her lip. She turns to Evelyn who is also biting her lip. A moment later, a tear makes its way from Evelyn's eye and travels down her cheek. When a tear begins to well in the other eye, Evelyn abruptly stands. "Excuse me," Evelyn whispers and quickly leaves the room.

Mrs. Gilbert faces the boy with a growing smile. "One burrito, comin' right up. Unless ya' want two. Ya hungry?

You want two?"

Angels peer downward on a pretend humanity of perfect dolls while other angels peer upward toward a perfect vision of heaven. Glass eyed girls in pretty dresses push baby-carriages that contain smiling babies. Porcelain boys with ragged straw hats sit on a shelf holding porcelain fishing poles. Velvet gowns, lace dresses, satin pajamas. Diamond tiaras, sun bonnets, plaid hats. Chubby fingers, rosy cheeks, plump faces. All with demure smiles. All with sparkling eyes. All wholesomely posed. All made to evoke a shopper's *"Ahhhh"* worth hundreds or thousands of dollars.

Seated on the edge of her canopy bed, Evelyn's eyes are red and her cheeks are wet with tears. She sniffles into a tissue. The painted eyes of angels keep watch on her with loving concern.

A knock comes to the door. It opens without waiting for Evelyn's response. Mrs. Gilbert enters, then quietly closes the door behind her. With her lip quivering, Evelyn watches the stocky woman cross the room and come sit beside her on the bed. The mattress gives and Evelyn leans into the large woman's side. "I can't get over it," Evelyn explains between sniffs. "He slept next to his mama. He slept on a grave." More tears fall from her eyes.

"I know." Mrs. Gilbert runs a comforting hand over Evelyn's back.

"He slept next to his mama," Evelyn repeats.

"I know."

"And he didn't want to dirty anything." Evelyn sniffs.

"I know."

"I can't get over that. I don't know what's happening to me. I just… It just… My heart, I just…"

"I know."

"Missus Gilbert, that was the sweetest, kindest, most lonely, most tragic, most beautiful, simplest thing I've ever heard of."

"It was."

"That little boy is messing me up. He spits food and his teeth are always covered with crap and he barely speaks English and he has that stupid smile…"

"Gets to ya, don't it?"

"It does. It really does." Evelyn wipes her eyes.

"Why don't you come on down for breakfast and finish your yogurt? I made éclairs yesterday special just for you."

"Éclairs?" Evelyn asks with childlike surprise. "For me?"

"To say thank you for taking Cincinnati out for ice cream and inviting Bernard to join you. It was almost like you were a real human being."

"Oh Missus Gilbert, that is so nice." Evelyn lifts her hand to touch the housekeeper's arm but withdraws it. With a nearly glowing smile on Evelyn's face and a pert little grin on Mrs. Gilbert's, they rise from the bed and walk from the room.

Cincinnati sits at the breakfast nook table digging in his ear with his finger. He is just beginning to examine the haul when Evelyn and Mrs. Gilbert enter. Evelyn dabs at her red-rimmed eyes. The boy wipes his finger on his pants, then sits up straight.

"You ready to eat?" Mrs. Gilbert asks as she heads for the pan on the stove. Evelyn carefully lowers herself into the chair opposite Cincinnati.

"I sure am. I'm starvin'." Cincinnati watches Evelyn pick up her spoon. Then making very little eye-contact, she cups the plastic yogurt container with her hand and begins

116

to take tiny bites. Cincinnati observes her pink eyes. "You okay?"

"Yes. Fine. Thank you," Evelyn answers with a minimal glance.

Mrs. Gilbert slides a plate with two burritos in front of the boy. "There ya go. Eat up." She heads back into the kitchen.

"You wouldn't believe what I got out a my ears this morning," Cincinnati brags, then savagely tears a bite from his burrito.

Evelyn gags at the yogurt on her spoon, then disdainfully places it back in the container. The housekeeper's ever-observant eyes take in the dilemma. She takes a small plate of éclairs over to Evelyn and removes the yogurt. "Unless he starts talkin' about poop, these might look a little more appetizin' to ya."

With a brief, yet slightly horrified smile, Evelyn takes one.

The boy chews with an open mouth. "Could y'all hear the coyotes last night? They got hold 'a somethin', what with all the yippin' and howlin', it was crazy loud out there. Sausalito had to be runnin' with 'em – happy as a lark I betcha."

"Do you at all realize what fell out of your mouth just now?" Evelyn shudders. "It's a wonder you don't starve to death. Eat or speak. I thought we covered this yesterday."

"Starve to death." Cincinnati laughs. "That's funny." A gregarious little boy smile with food-covered teeth follows.

Evelyn's eyes roll back while her nostrils flare. "It wasn't intended to be humorous." Evelyn raises an éclair, savors a tiny bite, then pats the corners of her mouth with a napkin. "These are so decadent."

"You talked with food in yer mouth!" The Sprinkler's exclamation is accompanied by a shower of particles as well as his pointing finger.

"Yet I sprayed nothing." Evelyn argues, then critically looks at the filthy ragamuffin. "We should vacuum you."

The boy smiles. Although he doesn't know what a vacuum is, it sounds funny.

"If you end up staying here, we'll have to invest in a tank of lye. We'll rig a cattle dipping apparatus by the door, then after the germs have been burned off, we'll hose you down before you enter the house. As I'm sitting here I can actually see dirt falling off of you."

Mrs. Gilbert watches the conversation from the sink with a smile on her face. When she turns on the water to rinse a pan, she glances out the window. *"Oh dear Lord,"* she cries. *"Call nine-one-one!"* She tosses the pan into the sink with a clatter, then rushes to the French doors.

Without calling 911 as instructed, Evelyn and Cincinnati rise and rush to follow her.

Sausalito staggers onto the patio soaked with blood. His clothes and skin are shredded. As a couple of concerned men from the landscaping crew approach him from behind, Mrs. Gilbert runs up to him. He reaches out for her, begins to say something, but his knees buckle and he collapses wordlessly into her arms. "Oh no. Oh no. Oh goodness," she cries. Between her and the workmen, they gently lower Sausalito onto the patio.

Cincinnati explodes into tears at the sight, then runs to his brother's side. "Sausalito! Sausalito," he yells but the eyes of his brother seem not to focus anywhere, much less on him.

Frozen just outside the French doors, Evelyn gasps, *"Oh my God."* She blinks twice, then runs back into the house.

"Evelyn, are you calling?" Mrs. Gilbert shouts and twists around. Seeing no one and getting no response, she leaves Sausalito and runs into the house. The phone sits in its cradle and Evelyn is no where in sight. "Damn that woman," Mrs. Gilbert curses and grabs the phone. After pushing the numbers, she yells toward the door. "Bring him in here, out of the sun!"

As the two laborers and Cincinnati carry Sausalito in through the doors, Mrs. Gilbert shouts into the phone. "Got an injured boy. Don't know what happened. He's lost a lot of blood and is torn to hell. He's goin' into shock. Twenty nineteen Happy Canyon Drive. Hurry!" She tosses the phone aside and no sooner rushes back to the boy, than a horn blares from somewhere out front.

"That was fast," one of the workmen comments.

"That can't be them." Mrs. Gilbert takes off for the front door in a lumbering trot. Just as she exits the kitchen, she meets Evelyn dashing toward her.

"I have the car out front. Carry him through," Evelyn instructs. When the workmen do not immediately move, Evelyn runs into the kitchen and picks up the teen's head. "Help me," she shouts. The men get their arms beneath the young man and lift him.

The entourage struggles through the mansion, then out the grand entry and down the steps to where the limousine sits waiting with the doors open. While the workmen carefully lay Sausalito onto the floor in the rear, Evelyn runs around and jumps in the driver's seat. Mrs. Gilbert yells, "Wait two seconds," dashes back into the mansion, then reappears an instant later. The moment she leaps into the car, its tires squeal against the cobbled drive. The workmen jump back, then watch as the heavy limousine careens out the gate and roars full throttle down the road.

"How is he?" Evelyn shouts over her shoulder.

"Hurry Missy, hurry," Mrs. Gilbert yells over Cincinnati's wailing. "I told you to call nine-one-one. Why didn't you call nine-one-one?"

"They always go to Happy Canyon Boulevard. They never get it right. I've called 'em enough times to know." Just then an ambulance screams through the intersection ahead on Happy Canyon Boulevard. "I didn't think we had the time."

"Good job. Good job. Where was Bernard?"

"He took the Bentley for an oil-change."

"Do you know where you're going?"

"I was at the E. R. for that hangnail last year. I know where to go."

"Oh Lordy! What a mess." Mrs. Gilbert begins to examine the teen. "Think I know what all the yippin' and howlin' was about last night."

"Pack must'a turned on him. Is he gonna die?" Cincinnati cries.

"Don't know. He's lost a lot of blood. Here, I gotta get his feet up." The portly housekeeper maneuvers herself so that she can lift Sausalito's feet up on her lap.

"We're getting him to help as fast as we can," Evelyn calls from the front. "We aren't gonna let him die." Evelyn grabs the wheel firmly as she spots several lanes of stopped traffic ahead. "Hang on back there."

Cincinnati and Mrs. Gilbert brace themselves.

The limousine bounces up over a curb to drive on the median, mowing down small trees and shrubs as it sails past the blockage of traffic. Then with its horn blaring and chunks of the front-end flying off or dragging along by sparking electrical wires, it hurtles off the curb and hits the pavement with a brutal bounce. Although horns blare and cars skid to avoid it, it careens through unscathed.

"Holy shit," Mrs. Gilbert yells.

"Woo hoo," Evelyn hollers gleefully. "Two blocks to go. How's he doing?" After an abrupt left turn and a few more vehicles skidding to avoid it, the limousine speeds up to the emergency entrance with its horn blaring.

Within moments, orderlies and nurses have pulled Sausalito out of the car and loaded him onto a gurney. As he's wheeled inside, Mrs. Gilbert wraps her arms around Evelyn. "That was some drivin' lady." Her big hand pats Evelyn's slight back with enough power to knock the wind out of her.

"Th – an - ank - yy - ou," Evelyn replies between pats. As soon as she's released from the hefty woman's arms, Evelyn kneels, takes Cincinnati's hand, and looks him deeply in the eye. "I think we got him here in time. He's going to be okay. Listen, you two go on in. I gotta move the car."

"Oh, wait," Mrs. Gilbert ducks back into the car, then comes back with a sheet of paper and a pen in her hands. "You're going to need this to get him treated." She hands the guardianship document and pen to Evelyn.

Evelyn looks at it, then at Cincinnati, and lays the paper on the hood of the car. With her lips sucked in, she writes her name and Carter's in the blank space and signs it. She hands it back to Mrs. Gilbert. "Tell them I'll be right in."

Sausalito sleeps under a light white sheet with a myriad of wires and IVs attached to him. Monitors softly beep and disclose his vitals.

Evelyn and Cincinnati sit at his side. "So, do you really think he's gonna be all right?" Cincinnati asks.

"He's gonna be fine," Evelyn confirms with a comforting smile. When Cincinnati's eyes go back to his brother, Evelyn looks down and flicks at the smears of crusted blood on the front of the fuzzy robe. Then she shifts her eyes to a wayward lock of hair that hangs over her face, raises her hand and pushes it back.

Cincinnati's layers of dirty clothing lie heaped in a pile on the floor. Evelyn checks the time. "I hope Missus Gilbert gets back with my clothes soon. I sure would like to eat something."

"No one's gonna care if yer in a robe," Cincinnati reasons. "Ever' one around here is sick or wearin' funny clothes already."

"I think your brother's dried blood might be a little disconcerting for others to see."

"What's dis-erting?"

"Unpleasant."

"You might could turn it inside-out."

"You might could learn to speak the English language."

Cincinnati looks at Evelyn's perfectly straight face for a moment, and then smiles broadly and begins to laugh. Evelyn chuckles a little, then reaches over and gently moves a wayward lock of hair away from one of Cincinnati's eyes.

"Are you gonna be our new mom?"

Evelyn shrugs. "I guess so."

Cincinnati nods solemnly. "So, you like us now?"

After another shrug, Evelyn opens her mouth, says nothing, then shrugs again.

Cincinnati looks over at Sausalito. "How long's he gonna sleep?"

"I imagine quite a while. He has a lot of healing to do and they've loaded him up with anesthesia and antibiotics."

"That ain't English."

"Yes it is. What do you know?"

Cass suddenly bursts through the door. Her heels pound the floor as she bee-lines it for the bed. "Oh the poor dear. How is he? Is he okay?"

"He's fine. Or at least he will be." Evelyn stands and places her hand gently on Cass's arm.

"How can you be so calm?" Cass reaches out and pulls up the sheet that covers the sleeping teen. She gasps, then raises her other hand to her mouth. "Oh dear God."

"They can't stitch him up because of the threat of infection. He's going to have to heal from the inside out. That means a lot of scars," Evelyn states matter-of-factly. "It took two pints of blood to fill him back up. His blood pressure was sixty over forty when we got him here."

Cass brings both of her hands to her mouth as the sheet she was holding silently wafts down onto Sausalito's body. "So he was almost…" Cass begins, then stops herself and looks at Cincinnati.

"We aren't saying the 'D' word," Evelyn interjects, "because he's going to be okay." She rubs Cincinnati's back reassuringly. "But you should have seen what he looked like before they cleaned him up. I honestly can't imagine how he made it back to us."

"Getting home is a powerful motivator," Cass says kindly, smiles, then wraps her arms around her best friend and hugs her tight. "I'm so proud of you. I am so, *so*, proud of you for what you did."

Cass abruptly releases her friend and lunges for Cincinnati. "Come here, big man!" She kneels, flings the young boy into her bosom, then smothers him into it. "Just when ya' think it's gotten as bad as it can get, it gets worse. I can't think of any more bad stuff that could possibly happen so things have got to start getting better." She pushes the breathless boy back and looks into his eyes. "How are you holding up?"

"I'm a little hungry."

"He's a little hungry." Cass spins on Evelyn. "This boy is hungry. *Did you hear that?*"

"Well, I'm waiting for Missus Gilbert," Evelyn begins to explain. "She took a cab home to go home and get clothes for me and..."

"...and then you'll have to get dressed and primp and we all know how long that takes and that's just to achieve mediocre. *Did you somehow not hear that this boy is hungry?* We have an emergency here, *Evelyn.* How about I take this gorgeous young man to lunch? Let me get him out in the sunlight and away from all this sterile depression for a few minutes."

Evelyn shrugs. "I suppose."

Then Cass rolls her eyes upward in thought and brings a finger to her chin. "Maybe we'll eat in the cafeteria downstairs. The way I flew over here, I'm pretty sure the cops are looking for me. There might actually be a helicopter involved because at one point, my commute over here was kind of like a car chase and I may have stretched the parameters of how many directions cars can go on one-way streets a couple of times. I'm hoping they track me here because I parked next to the limousine. Once they see that wreck, I'm pretty sure they'll forget about my seventy-five in a thirty and that hot dog vendor's cart. Did you know there is actually a tree stuck in your suspension?"

Evelyn shrugs.

"Yeah, that's the plan," Cass confirms. "Me and my little dream man here will go into hiding until the heat turns on you. Is that rude? I don't think it is. Anyway..." Cass rolls her eyes upward to find the thought that will complete her devious plan. "If anyone asks, the Carrera was stolen by a strikingly beautiful woman that definitely wasn't me. How I got here, I don't know.

"We'll be back soon but don't wait up if we're not." Cass stands, then begins to pull Cincinnati from the room. "I may succumb to this little man's charms and whisk him away to my tree house in Bolivia to begin a highly improper relationship."

"I don't want to go to 'Livia. I jus' want me a hamburger," Cincinnati timidly says.

Both women freeze.

He looks at their stunned faces. "Is a hamburger a bad thing like the Walmarts?" he asks sheepishly.

"Are you kidding?" Cass slaps her ass. "I didn't get this munching down on salads. Hamburgers it is." Cass has one foot in the hall when she turns back to her friend. "Did I mention how beautiful you look today?"

With mussed hair, a bloodstained robe and absolutely no makeup, Evelyn smiles graciously.

Cincinnati squirms out of Cass's grip, walks back to the bed, leans over his brother and whispers, "I'll be right back. Don't you worry about nothin'. You'll be fine." He kisses him on the cheek, then turns around and blinks his large, innocent eyes.

Both women look at him. Cass turns to Evelyn. "So, *so* proud of you." Cass then blows a kiss to Evelyn, grabs the boy's hand and yanks him along.

As he is being pulled down the hall, Cincinnati looks up at Cass. "Where's 'Livia?"

"It's Bolivia, a lush green country in South America with wild monkeys and sloths and exotic birds."

"You gots you a real tree house there?"

"I actually do," Cass exclaims with a wave of her arm. "I built it myself – well, me and a smoking hot young – but still of age – barely – but who's counting – Mexican caballero that I picked up in Tijuana – but never mind that little detail and the forty-two nights of wild jungle, howler monkey... Um, anyway, that's just crazy that I actually have a tree house in Bolivia, isn't it?"

Sausalito lies awake in a strange and sterile room looking around at his surroundings in the semi-light of morning. Cincinnati is sound asleep on a cot placed next to his bed. On the other hospital bed, lays an unidentifiable form under a mound of covers and pillows. A crease forms on Sausalito's forehead, then deepens as he looks around some more.

The nurse who enters the room to check Sausalito's vitals smiles broadly to find him awake. "Well, look who's up," she chirps to greet him. "Did you sleep well last night?"

Opting to say nothing, Sausalito watches with utmost apprehension as the nurse checks the readouts on the machines.

"I heard you had a run-in with some wild animals," she continues brightly. "How are you feeling this morning?"

"Not so good," Sausalito croaks.

Cincinnati stirs from his slumbers, slips his legs out of the blankets, and sits up as he wipes sleep from his eyes.

"Am I in a hospital?" the teen asks.

"You sure are," The nurse answers.

Sausalito turns to Cincinnati. "Hey, little brother."

"Hey, Sausalito."

"That's a wonderful name; Sausalito. All us nurses have been talking about it. I bet you could stand to use the bathroom this morning." The nurse maneuvers the IV so that Sausalito can wheel it along with him. "Pull this along with you. It needs to stay attached."

Sausalito nods, then pulls off the sheet that covers

him. He immediately pulls it back over. His eyes are now wide open. "What the heck am I wearin'?"

"Not much. You're going to feel a draft. We promise not to look. Let me know if you need help."

Sausalito looks back at the nurse, horrified.

"I'm a nurse. There is literally nothing I haven't seen, or unfortunately, haven't touched."

Even more appalled, Sausalito sits, then cautiously stands. He holds the gown together behind him with one hand while he pulls the IV with the other and backs toward the bathroom. After he closes the door, the nurse chuckles lightly. "And how are you this morning?" she asks Cincinnati.

"I sleeped real good," he replies. "Thanks for making my brother better."

"Oh, you're welcome, sweetheart. Personally, I didn't do much more than check on him, but I'll pass it on. We don't get many thank yous."

Then looking toward the mound of blankets on the other bed, the nurse inquires, "How is your mother?"

"Oh, she's dead."

The nurse takes a couple quick steps toward the mound of blankets before Cincinnati realizes the misunderstanding. "Oh, that ain't my mama. That's the lady. She's takin' care of us now."

"I thought that was your mother."

"No. Mama died last week."

"I am so sorry."

Cincinnati shrugs.

The bathroom door opens and Sausalito emerges fuming mad. "Me an' Snarl are gonna have us a talk," he angrily asserts. "They must 'a bit me a hundred times!"

"What happened to Fang?" Cincinnati asks as if it was an old classmate.

"Guess he must 'a died. Snarl never did cotton to me much. Guess he's leadin' the pack now. At first he seemed okay, then he turnt on me. All the others joined him. I should 'a had a club with me. I'd 'a fixed his wagon."

The mound of covers on the occupied bed begin to stir. With her hair standing all directions, Evelyn's head groggily emerges.

Sausalito blinks. *"What's she doin' here?"*

"Takin' care of us," Cincinnati answers simply.

After a mistrustful glare at Evelyn, Sausalito wordlessly makes his way back to his bed. He's about to get in when he shakes the IV stand. "What in tarnation is this here thing?"

"That is an intravenous antibiotic."

"A what? Unhook it. I ain't stayin' here."

"Oh yes you are." Evelyn suddenly flings her covers aside. Pillows fall to the floor as she comes to her feet. When Sausalito starts to pick at the tape that holds the line to his arm, she marches his direction. "You leave that right where it is."

His eyes bore into hers. "Joneses don't stay in no hospitals."

"You stubborn little man. You leave that alone and get back in that bed," Evelyn yells.

"I ain't doin' it and you don't tell me what to do."

"*STOP IT*," Cincinnati screams. All eyes turn to him. "You almos' died, big brother. You almos' left me all alone in the world. That lady saved yer life and wrecked up one 'a her fancy cars doin' it. She stayed with us all night." A tear wells up in Cincinnati's eye and runs down his cheek. "Mama put us where she did for a reason an' she left that paper for a reason. The lady and Carter is our guardians now so you do what she says an' git back in yer bed."

An orderly pops in the door, concerned at the

commotion. With an expression now slightly subdued, Sausalito looks quickly at all the faces that are looking back at him, pats the tape back in place on his arm, then sits on the bed. He pulls his legs up, then lies down. The nurse reaches across and pulls his blanket into place. After folding his arms over his chest, Sausalito stares at the ceiling and sets his jaw.

The nurse cautiously mentions, "Breakfast will be coming in about twenty minutes. The doctor has started rounds. He should be here shortly." Getting no acknowledgement from the belligerent teen, she faces Evelyn. "Will you be all right?"

"We'll be fine," Evelyn assures and the nurse steps out. Evelyn looks at the young man stubbornly staring at the ceiling. She sighs. "I put Carter's and my names on the guardianship papers your mother left. You might not be happy about it, but it's done and that's the way it is."

"You don't like us," Sausalito states bluntly. "You didn't want us in yer house. You didn't even want Missus Gilbert feedin' us. You think we're jus' hillbillies an' filthy an' stupid."

Evelyn reaches over, touches Sausalito's hand and admits, "You're right. I did."

The stubborn, angry eyes shift to look at Evelyn.

"I don't know what happened. I don't know why I signed that paper. All I can tell you is that it felt right and it still does. What I thought about you was wrong, Sausalito.

"I was wrong."

Chapter Nine

You said Home

"Thank you so much," Evelyn repeats for the fifth time to the nurses at the station. The clock reads 8:30 A.M. With Cincinnati obediently waiting at her side, she adds, "We're going home to make ourselves presentable. We'll be back this evening to visit. If my little wolf man gives you any more problems, call me."

"Will do, Missus Chatsblythe," a nurse responds. "He'll be fine. Don't worry about a thing."

Evelyn parts with a polite smile, hair unabashedly still askew and her clothing rumpled from the overnight. As she walks toward the elevator, Cincinnati runs ahead to push the button. He proudly turns to Evelyn. "I knows how to do this an' I likes me a elevator."

Evelyn winces. "We's gotta learn us some English."

Cincinnati smiles gregariously. When the elevator dings and the doors open, Evelyn returns his smile. Then with a warm sparkle in her eyes, adds, "I likes me a elevator, too."

From what is becoming his place in the front seat of the Bentley, Cincinnati observes a plethora of exclusive galleries and elegant boutiques in awe as Bernard drives them along a boulevard rife with sidewalk cafés. The boy abruptly twists around to face Evelyn who is rides alone in the back seat. "Can we go to McDonald's for breakfast?"

"No," Bernard answers for the mistress. "I've seen you eat. We're in the Bentley. We'd have to put you in a rubber sack to get you home."

"I'm getting better," Cincinnati replies.

"He actually is," Evelyn agrees. "He only spit out half his dinner last evening." She and Bernard's eyes meet in the mirror. The chauffer's eyes narrow and his nostrils flare. Evelyn shrugs, then sighs. "Cincinnati, I'll have to agree with Bernard on this one. Besides, Missus Gilbert has already stenched up the house making your breakfast. We'll get McDonald's another time when I'm driving my car."

"Not the Aston," Bernard whines.

Evelyn raises her nose. "It's *my* car. And don't worry, we'll not take it to go."

He shudders. "I'll be putting a box of wet-wipes in all the vehicles. And a roll of paper towels."

"Good idea." Evelyn winks at the chauffer via the mirror.

They both smile easily.

As Evelyn sunbathes in a bikini beside the sparkling pool, Cincinnati wanders near, then sighs heavily. "I'm kind of bored."

Evelyn looks toward a watch sitting on the table beside her that is barely past two o'clock. "Why don't you take a nap?" She reclines and closes her eyes as if the subject is closed – which it most likely is not.

"Ain't tired and naps is for babies." (Told you so.)

"Why don't you help Floyd?"

"He's takin' a nap."

"Help Bernard then." Evelyn flicks her fingers the direction she hopes Cincinnati will wander off to.

"He says he has errands to run and I can't come 'cause

he needs to be able to think an' I ask too many questions."

"How about Missus Gilbert?"

"She said to come see you. She said don't take no for an answer 'cause I'm yer respons-a-built-ee, not hers." The boy remains standing at Evelyn's side and patiently observes her serenely closed eyes.

Evelyn puckers her lips, but her eyes remain closed. "I need some alone time. Could I have a half hour and then I'll shower and we'll go for ice cream?"

"One a yer showers lasts a whole hour. Since now you done adopted us, now you gotta put me in school. Mister Bartel said so. I wanna go look at a school. I ain't never seen a school."

"Dear God." Evelyn sighs. "Will you *please* go away? Give me fifteen blessed minutes. Can I have fifteen minutes? I slept like crap last night. Hospital linens must be made of either polyester or burlap. If there is a difference, it's beyond me what it is. I'll tell you what it was *not*. It was *not* Egyptian cotton with a six hundred thread count.

"The mattress was a lump comprised of other lumps with a base of what had to be plywood. I listened to carts banging and doors shutting and people coming in and out all hours of the night. I slept all of ten minutes and even then it was like camping in the Arctic Circle. Apparently hospitals don't pay their utility bills. Could I possibly have fifteen blessed minutes to clear my mind?"

"You complain a lot."

"So do you."

"I thought you cleared yer mind when ya did yogurt."

"*Yoga* didn't help. *Yogurt* is something you eat. Go to your room and play."

"Don't have nothin' to play with. My stick done got blowed up."

"Your one and only toy was a stick?" Evelyn opens one

of her serenely closed eyes.

"Pokin' stick. Fer when ya find somethin' dead."

"Why don't you go meander through the woods and locate another stick?" Evelyn raises her hand and flicks her fingers in the general direction of the hillside. "Surely something has expired and you can poke its corpse."

"A pokin' stick is special. You have to carve it. I needs me a knife. Can I gets me a knife?"

"You can gets you a vocabulary. You aren't going to leave me alone, are you?"

"Prob'ly not."

After releasing a very deep sigh, Evelyn opens her other serenely closed eye and pulls herself up to a sitting position. She looks at Cincinnati and sighs one more time. "I must look into hiring a nanny."

"What's a nanny?"

"It's essentially a midget wrangler," Evelyn explains as she stands. "I suspect having one will preserve my sanity and prevent your premature demise. How about I put on a huddled masses disguise and we'll go to one of those Walmart places? I think there are no less than a million of them so it shouldn't be too hard to find one."

"Are you serious?" Cincinnati gapes. "You'll takes me to Walmarts?"

"It's the only thing I can do without first bathing. My odor can be part of my disguise. Possibly I could walk like a hunchback in order to blend in. You can select a cart full of toys and coloring books and balls and such. Then we'll purchase a lock for the *outside* of your door. I had no idea how taxing all this would be."

"What about school?"

"Honestly? Can you not be happy with a cart full of toys? I absolutely cannot face the prospect of enrolling you in school just yet. Have I not had enough traumas over the past few days? Dealing with the public education system will likely finish me off. With English being your second language, I imagine you'll be placed with the idiots in remedial courses. Hopefully they can teach you how not to slobber." Evelyn shudders, then points sternly. "We're getting toys. Nothing else. No more requests. No more bugging. I'm going to change into my disguise right now and then we'll go."

"Can we get us some ice creams?"

As he is eating dinner at the dining room table, Cincinnati runs miniature toy cars around his place setting and an invasion of plastic dinosaurs. Having finished their meal, Carter and Evelyn watch him intently. "So," Carter begins with a teasing smile, "will going to the Walmart be a weekly excursion for the two of you?"

Although Cincinnati looks up with an excited and breathless smile, Evelyn rubs her temples. "It will not. I likely will have nightmares of tattooed women overflowing their halter tops and large people driving carts who bump people out of their way and then give them the finger." She lays her hands on the table. "Carter, I saw things today that eyes should never have to see and most of them involved hot pink Spandex."

"I hear ya, hon. I hear ya."

"There ought to be a warning label on their doors or a documentary on PBS. It was a hideous experience."

"I hear ya." Carter pats her hand affectionately. "Other than that, how was day two of motherhood?"

With a flare of her nostrils, Evelyn looks dryly at Cincinnati's hopeful smile, then confesses, "It was wonderful."

"Really?"

"Well, apparently I complain a lot. I also don't really know how a mother is supposed to act or what one should do in any given circumstance. A couple times I nearly called nine-one-one to pull me out of a panic attack. I thought I might have to breathe in a paper bag until I calmed down, but we got through it." She and Cincinnati smile affectionately at one another.

"Wow," Carter marvels.

Mrs. Gilbert enters the dining room wearing a Nerf shoulder holster and loaded weapon. She and Cincinnati dangerously narrow their eyes at one another and slowly tilt their heads back in the strained greeting of sworn enemies. Cincinnati pats his hip holster with its locked and loaded weapon. Mrs. Gilbert sneers at her nemesis, then begins to gather the dishes. The potentially volatile situation is observed wryly by both Carter and Evelyn.

"Well, I imagine we need to head to the hospital for visiting hours." Carter scoots his chair back, deposits his napkin near his plate and stands.

"No dessert?" Mrs. Gilbert questions. "I made a peach cobbler."

"I bet Sausalito would love some of that." Carter ponders a moment, then turns to Evelyn. "Do they allow outside food, or do you think we could sneak it in?"

Evelyn pats her lips with her napkin. "I don't see why we couldn't bring it."

"Will Cass be there tonight?" Cincinnati asks hopefully. "I likes her. She's funny."

"No, sweetie," Evelyn replies. "Only family tonight. We need to help your brother get used to the idea of us being his family."

"Okay." The boy shrugs. "Kin I show him some 'a the stuff I got today?"

"He'll probably make a face and say it's of the Devil."

Cincinnati twists his mouth to the side. "Prob'ly."

"I'll cut up the cobbler and put it in containers for

you," Mrs. Gilbert offers as she carries dirty dishes back toward the kitchen.

"Okay but remember to take off your..." Evelyn waves her hand at Mrs. Gilbert's gun and shoulder holster. "Security will tackle you in the hallway if you go in armed like that. And you might as well bring the whole cobbler and paper plates. There's a Starbucks in the building so you won't have to bring a beverage."

Without noticing the housekeeper's confused expression, Evelyn turns, bends and begins to help Cincinnati gather up his toys. She speaks softly to the boy. "Why don't you put a few of these in your pockets anyway, just in case your brother's in a good mood and wants to see them?"

Carter looks at the housekeeper who has not moved and still stands in the doorway with the same stunned expression. "Well, you heard the lady, get rid of those dishes and let's get going. Only family tonight." He winks and smiles.

Mrs. Gilbert looks back at Carter, pulls the corners of her mouth down, then nods.

Parked near the front steps of the mansion are the family's Bentley, Carter's Ferrari, Raymond's black Mercedes and Cass's yellow Carrera. The front door of the mansion is adorned with balloons, streamers, and a banner that says *Welcome Home Sausalito!*

Sausalito sits alone atop the landscaped knoll at his mother's graveside while everyone else sits around waiting for him on the festively decorated patio. Conversation in the group is mostly subdued but Carter's is non-existent. His eyes shift between the motionless teen on the top of the knoll and his watch as the minute hand continues to advance. "He said a few minutes," Carter complains to

Cincinnati. "Does that mean something different in your world than it does in ours?"

"Naw. He's bein' difficult. You want I should go git him?"

"No. I'll do it," Carter offers, then turns to Mrs. Gilbert. "Go ahead and bring out the food. We're eating in five minutes. If he doesn't come back down with me, we're eating without him."

"But it's his party," Cincinnati argues. "We can't eat without him."

"We can if he wants to sit up there and ignore us," Carter retorts, then begins to walk toward the knoll.

"Come on Cincinnati." Evelyn places her hand gently on the boy's shoulder. "Let's help Missus Gilbert bring the food out."

"Okay. I likes me to help."

"Too bad you don't likes you to speak English. The work *like* does not ever have an 'S' on the end of it."

"What about if I say that Cass likes me?" Cincinnati says smartly, then looks up to Evelyn as they walk into the house.

"Fine," Evelyn concedes. "Then the word *like* is never used as a plural and only has an 'S' on the end of it when used in the form of an active or possessive verb or some such nonsense. That is beside the point. How do you not hear that it sounds ignorant to say things like: I likes me a – I don't know – toad or whatever it is that people like you like?"

"You always say things like, 'How do you not?' and 'How is it that you don't?' That sounds a little stupid, too. An' I do likes me a toad."

"Don't worry about me," Evelyn counters with an arrogant tone. "Worry about you and why you like toads."

137

Carter climbs the winding stone steps to the top of the knoll, stops at the top, then waits for Sausalito to acknowledge him. "Everyone's waiting on you," he says when the teen's eyes meet his. "We'd like to eat."

"I ain't hungry."

"Then come and sit at the table and don't eat anything. Everyone is here for you and they're waiting on you. You need to appreciate that and come down and be considerate of other people's time, the effort they put into this, and the fact that other people might be hungry even if you're not." Carter places his hands on his hips.

Sausalito's already stony expression hardens further.

"I didn't ask for no *Welcome Home* party."

"Tough shit. You got one."

"This ain't my home and you an' the lady ain't my folks." Sausalito's voice rises. "I's only here 'cause I got no place else to go."

"Alright." Carter puckers his lips, nods his head ever so slightly and raises his eyebrows. "You should know that I only do diplomacy so long before I get my guns. I just picked up a figurative gun so here it is: our lives collided. Neither of us asked for this, but my wife and I have fed you, opened our home, gotten you a lawyer, preserved your mother's grave, paid for your medical care and even saved your life. Just because we *ain't* what you think we should be, doesn't mean we didn't do what we should have and more."

"I didn't like that Mrs. Gilbert said that yer wife, 'Would'a lifted a car to save her boy over there.' An' then she pointed at me. I ain't yer boy and yer wife ain't my mama," Sausalito states bluntly. "An' she ain't Cincinnati's neither even though she's actin' like it all of a time." He points at the mansion. "An' that ain't our home."

"We're trying to celebrate that you're alive and well

and you're getting stuck on the semantics of whether this house is really your home or if your guardians are really your parents. Why don't you quit worrying about what we aren't and start appreciating what we are?"

"It ain't the truth."

Carter sighs, squints and points at the patio below. "You need to get your ass down there. Right. Fucking. Now."

Sausalito stands.

"Move it." Carter's still-pointing finger directs the belligerent teen down the stone staircase.

Sausalito's lip curls and a low growl begins in his throat.

"Are you actually growling at me?"

The growl becomes louder.

"Okay. Fine. You want to stay up here. Stay. Starve. Sleep up here. I don't care. If you can't appreciate what we're offering and you want to live and act like an animal, so be it." With that, Carter turns and stomps down the stone steps.

Three seconds later Carter is back atop the knoll. "This home isn't exactly the projects. Evelyn and I are decent people. I highly doubt you are going to do better than us. But whatever. I don't care." He stomps down the steps.

Four seconds later he's back again. "I know that all this must be very difficult for you. I sympathize. Your mother died. We know you loved her. We know she loved you and your brother. No one will ever replace her. I know you're hurt. I know you've lost everything. I know this isn't the way you want to live or even think you should live. I know all that. Problem is – you want to go backwards when your only option is to go forward. I'm not going to tip-toe around you. I'm not going to watch what I say or how I say it. So whatever. Stay up here. I don't care." After another frustrated wave of his arms, Carter disappears down the steps.

He's back almost immediately. "My wife has done and is doing something that amazes me. And she is doing of this because of you. She is doing this because of your brother. My wife does not do the things she's done the past few days. She's becoming a different person because of you and your brother and I like the person you boys are causing her to become. Meet us halfway. That's all I'm asking."

The two men stare at one another with eyes that are beginning to soften.

"I'm sorry," Sausalito says before Carter can leave again. He rolls his eyes, sighs, then takes a few difficult steps to approach Carter and look him in the eye. "I know you and yer wife is tryin' to be good to us." A single tear makes its way down Sausalito's cheek. "That *Welcome Home* sign and the balloons and all those smiling people kind of got to me. It felt like a lie. Like you's all lying to us."

"I can understand that." Carter nods. "Did you know your brother slept on your mother's grave the night you left?"

Sausalito looks down, wipes his eyes, sniffs, then nods. "He tol' me."

"Evelyn isn't trying to replace your mother but maybe she could be *a* mother. Even if you aren't there yet, can you let your brother have someone to care for him *like* a mother?"

Sausalito lifts one shoulder and tilts his head toward it. "I s'pose I could do that."

"Sorry I got so mad."

"Me too."

"I'm kind of used to getting my way. I tell people what

to do and they do it." Carter chuckles softly to himself. "But I guess maybe I've met my match."

Sausalito smiles, chuckles a little himself, then nods.

Carter extends his hand. Although Sausalito looks at it warily, he takes it and they shake. "You ready to come down?" Carter asks.

Sausalito looks over at his mother's grave – which at present is merely a level, barren spot in the middle of the knoll. "Is that how that's gonna look – jus' a patch of dirt?"

"I'm leaving her grave unfinished so you and your brother can decide what you want. The landscaper will come back and finish it however you want."

Sausalito faces Carter with uncertain eyes.

"It just can't look like a grave. The neighbors and the authorities would have a meltdown if they knew there was a cemetery here." Carter smiles. "You boys decide what you want and we'll do it." He raises a hand which he places on Sausalito's shoulder. The two nod, then walk down the steps together.

With a new day dawned and a full breakfast waiting on his plate, Cincinnati complains, "Why can't I go?"

"You're going to see your first movie today," Carter counters.

"I wants to go with you an' Sausalito."

"This is just he and I," Carter explains while tying the shoelace of his hiking boot. "I told him I wanted to do this hike as soon as he felt up to it. Last night he said he'd give it a go this morning. We're trying to bond and he and I need to do these things in order to make that happen."

"It isn't fair."

"Well, what can I say? Life isn't fair. Tough shit."

After blinking a couple times, Cincinnati turns to

Evelyn who has been observing their conversation with a bemused smile. The boy points at Carter. "He said tough shit."

"He says that," Evelyn explains, then forces her smile into remission. "I've heard him say it at work. In meetings. Even to his board of directors. If Mister Chatsblythe can say that to them, he can probably say it to you."

"It's not fair. None a this is fair."

With Carter following, Sausalito leads the way up the exposed scar on the canyon wall where the sliver of earth had torn through. It's a clear Saturday morning under a flawless blue sky. The sun is pounding their backs and sweat is pouring from their brows. Halfway up the hillside, they edge across a newly exposed outcropping of rock to get to a clump of shrubs that still cling to the broken hillside. They settle into its miniscule shade and break out water bottles. The magnificent estates that line Happy Canyon Drive weave along the valley floor below.

"You know, I've lived here five years and have never climbed up this ridge," Carter confesses. "It's a beautiful view – at least in my opinion."

"The lights is kind of pretty at night. Mama weren't one for electricity, but even she liked 'em."

"You know there's talk of developing this valley more. Some folks want to develop up here on the ridge as well. Of course the landslide might have cooled that notion some. Unfortunately, some day this view will be all rooftops." Carter snorts to himself. "That's a shame. I guess I understand a little more how you must feel about us outsiders ruining your paradise."

"Yeah, but I guess there ain't much I can do about it." Sausalito shrugs. He ponders the view. "This is nice, you an' me doin' this."

"It is."

"It didn't make my brother none too happy." Sausalito breaks a grin. "You tol' him tough shit. That made me laugh when he tol' me. You city people got some funny expressions."

"I may not be a representative sample." Carter laughs. "I can be a little blunt." Carter looks up at the blazing sun. "This day isn't getting any cooler. Shall we hit it?"

"I s'pose."

After scaling the remainder of the scar and coming at last to the top of the ridge, the two men again find a particle of shade to rehydrate under. Their view has more than doubled. "Wow," Carter marvels. "Did you have this view from your place?"

"Some 'a it. There was scrub in the way. Didn't used ta be this hard to get up here. The path I made used to run across zig-zag," Sausalito points out a portion of a footpath still visible at the edge of the sheared bank.

"I see. Still, that was a hell of a hike. I imagine that rosebush got heavy after a while."

Another grin spreads across the teen's face. "You noticed that, huh?"

"I noticed it. Given the circumstances, I wasn't going to say anything. It was a beautiful thing you did for your mother. I'm not gonna mind something like that."

"She loved roses. You want to see our pond? We had us a good pond up here."

"Sure. I'd love to see that."

They resume their hike, eventually making their way to undisturbed terrain. As they are walking down a well worn trial, Sausalito stops, sniffs, then turns toward a rabbit that peers back at him as it munches from a leafy patch of vegetation. Sausalito freezes.

Carter observes his companion and the situation

warily. *"You hunting?"* he whispers.

"I ain't up to that. Don't imagine neither yer wife ner Missus Gilbert would want me bringin' one 'a them home to gut, skin an' cook no how."

"You said *home*," Carter observes.

The teen's head angles. He looks away from Carter's eyes, then smiles a slight bit. "The pond's right yonder." He resumes leading the way with his long, slow gait.

In a couple minutes time, they stand together on the bank of small green pond set amidst the trees. "All the ground slopes in toward it." Sausalito points out. "That's how we manage to keeps it full."

"You actually drank this water?"

"Mama bought chlorine to put in it. Said it would make us sick if'n we didn't. I once made a thing out'a pipes an' that tub over yonder that we could fill up water an' then it'd come out the faucets. It broke an' I needed parts but Mama wouldn't let me get 'em. I like parts. That's the one thing I didn't like about Mama's ways. She didn't want me tinkerin'. Said I took after my daddy – tinkerin' all 'a time. She wanted me to be a thinker, not a tinker. That was her joke."

"You never said what happened to your father."

"Got kilt. I remember him some but I was little. I kinda think I got it pieced together, what happened to him. I remember we had electric way back when. I seen a television before. I know I did. I remember me a white building. Seemed it was somewhere around here. Don't know where it is. I've looked for it but never have found it. I remember watchin' my daddy tinker on a workbench. He'd explain stuff to me. He had ideas, big ideas. Mama jus' smiled about it all and rolt her eyes when he went on like he did. Then one day somethin' bad happened an' Daddy went away. I remember Mama goin' ta visit him

144

ever' day. I think we had us a car. We must a. And then she stopped. That's when she started sayin' things was of the Devil. Said we was never to take her to no hospital so I think our papa died in a hospital. I think it was because of some accident that happened from somethin' he was makin'. She never would say. Just told us we was better off without things of the Devil and tinkerin'."

"I'm sorry that happened."

"Ain't nothin' can be done about it."

"Still, it was obviously very painful to her."

Sausalito nods.

"Your mama would probably call me a tinkerer. My business is making prototypes of new inventions. You know what a prototype is?"

"No sir."

"It's a model of the first of its kind. Say a manufacturer wants to develop a new product. We do their research and development and engineer the best design. We also take existing products and engineer how to make them more efficient."

"That's right up my alley," Sausalito brightens. "I'm always thinkin' like that."

"You know, my business is rather high-tech — that means complicated electronics and computerization and all — you may not understand it, but I'd love to show you what I do sometime."

Sausalito nods, then looks away with a slight smile on his lips. He looks back and grins. "There's something you should probably know. I may not be up to date on the modern world, but Cincinnati and I have read Steinbeck, Hemmingway, Rand, Shakespeare and Tolstoy. We know verbs and adverbs, nouns and pronouns, proper syntax and all about double negatives. We know algebra, geometry and I've started trig. Don't even get me started on physics.

Mama was serious about our education."

Carter's head pulls back.

"But Mama gave us an identity. She told us who we ought to be. She told us not to compromise nor accept the ways of the world just because it was the way of the world. I'm not stupid and I understand a lot more than you think I do."

"Wow."

"Your identity is business, sophistication and wealth. Evelyn's is her appearance. Mine is hillbilly. Mama said we all hide behind something. We all act how we're expected to act because that's how society works."

"Wow."

"With Mama gone, I need to decide who I'm gonna be. I'm working on it, Carter. I'll let you know when I know. But, uh, until then, this will be our little secret."

"Wow."

Sausalito's eyes shift, then narrow to slits. He raises his head, then sniffs the very slight breeze that has just shifted. His eyes lock onto something and a crooked smile spreads across his face. "I knowed he was up here somewhere. I sensed it." The teen raises his arm and points toward a tree across the pond. "You see that over there, up in the tree, that tail hangin' down?"

Carter leans close to Sausalito to follow his pointed finger. A long tail that hangs down from a tree branch twitches. "Look over and up a little to yer lef'. You see them eyes lookin' back at ya?"

"Holy shit."

"That there's Kitty. We have us a understanding."

"Is that the puma you wrestled?"

"That's him."

"Holy shit."

"You city folk and yer sayin's." Sausalito shakes his

head wryly. "Ain't no shit holy and ain't no shit tough. Shit is shit."

While Carter's yet looking at the teen with amazement, Sausalito swats him on the back. "Come on, I'll show ya where me an' Cincinnati once built us a fort out a sticks an' mud when we was little. We was so proud a our fort... an' it's still standin', well somewhat, anyway."

Chapter Ten

I Can't Take You Anywhere

City lights spread out beneath the windows of a penthouse restaurant. A string quartet plays from a low stage fifty feet away from Carter and Evelyn's table. She is stunning. Simple pearl pendants dangle from her ears. A single strand of pearls punctuates her graceful neck. Her hair is up in a stylish knot. Black velvet caresses her slender figure all the way down to the straps of her black heels. However impressive Carter's proportioned physique and charcoal suit with a black silk shirt may be, he will never be noticed with Evelyn at his side.

Colorful bits of food artistically placed beneath drizzles of bold sauces adorn the white china plates set before them. The couple savors the flavors of their meal between deep gazes into one another's eyes. Carter raises a crystal glass of fine wine to take a sip but his eyes never leave Evelyn. "Your beauty has always amazed me but the radiance you exude tonight just takes my breath away."

Evelyn shyly swallows her food, then smiles sweetly and lowers her gaze.

"Oh my God," Carter melts. "That. What you did just now – I feel like I'm seventeen. I just about can't stand to be across this table from you."

Her demure laugh makes it worse.

"Am I the luckiest guy in the world?" he asks.

"I guess you are tonight."

"I guess I am."

Longing gazes replace their conversation.

Then to make their intimate moment complete, Evelyn ponders, "I wonder how the boys are."

Carter's loud laugh turns a few heads from the tables around them. Although he chokes it back, he looks back at Evelyn and laughs some more.

"Carter," Evelyn gently chides and brings a finger to her lips to shush him.

He leans close with dancing eyes. "Would you listen to you? That is just great. Wondering how the boys are right in the middle of a moment like this. That is so great."

Evelyn leans forward and whispers confidentially. "You know Cincinnati wanted to come along and pestered me all day."

"I'm sure he did."

"He doesn't really understand why he couldn't."

"No, not at all," Carter observes. "He's totally gotten into your heart."

Evelyn shrugs. "That goofy smile. I cannot resist that disgusting goofy smile."

Carter spears a bite with his fork, then raises it to her lips. "Try this."

"Oh. That is wonderful," she exclaims when she tastes it. "You have to try this." Evelyn gathers a sample from her plate.

"Oh, yeah. That's the stuff." Carter rolls his eyes back and imitates a dog's reaction to a good scratching.

"I have three men I cannot take anywhere."

"That you do."

"Am I the luckiest girl in the world?"

"I guess you are tonight." Carter gazes at Evelyn. "You know the black dress song where the couple forgoes their long-awaited dinner to…" he glances around, then looks back at her, raises a nostril, snarls mischievously and growls lowly.

Evelyn laughs more loudly than she'd anticipated. When a few more heads turn, she places a couple fingers on her lips in embarrassment. "I guess I can't take myself anywhere either."

"This is the best date we've had in a long time."

"It is. I haven't even complained about anything."

Carter's ever-present smile goes into maintenance mode. His eyes continue to sparkle.

Evelyn pats his hand. "I guess I'm not bored anymore. I have actual real-life things on my plate these days."

They look down at the bits of exotic morsels on their plates, then laugh at the absurdity.

"I'd love me a chicken-fried steak with mashed potatoes and gravy," Carter confides.

"Or maybe squirrel," Evelyn suggests with mock excitement.

"Chicken-fried squirrel," Carter muses with a finger brought to his chin. "Now that sounds tasty."

Unfortunately, his timing could not have been worse.

The regal Mrs. Taylor Alexander (the third) with the hide of a dead something draped over her shoulders had diverted her grand entry, deigning to stop at the Chatsblythe's table in order to offer a charitable greeting – or something along those lines – perhaps. Carter looks up like a guilty child at a set of eyes that peer disapprovingly at him down a long, but quite aristocratic nose. Mrs. Taylor Alexander blinks a couple times with the kind of stunned disbelief that is the exclusive domain of the 1% of the 1% or the .01% - which just doesn't have a good ring to it and will probably never catch on. Carter's crude suggestion earns him a very long and somewhat exasperated sigh along with a slight roll of the aristocratic eyes. Mrs. T.A. III then turns to Evelyn. "My dear Evelyn, you look positively beautiful tonight."

"Why, thank you Alexis." Evelyn smiles graciously.

The regal nose, followed by the regal chin, rise, then angle ever-so-slightly to the left. A jewel-encrusted length of gold rope with jewel encrusted tendrils radiating from its arc, hangs around Alexis' slightly-more-than-middle-aged neck. Mr. Taylor Alexander (the third) stands meekly behind his fortress of a wife and says nothing. Alexis extends her neck further and raises her eyes and nose higher. Evelyn abruptly bumps around in her seat to curiously peer the direction of Alexis' regal eyes. With both of them now feigning to look at a non-existent something which is apparently across the room and near the ceiling, Alexis abandons her ruse. She huffs. Evelyn turns toward the aristocrat with wide, innocent eyes. "We missed you at the women's tea," Alexis sniffs. "News of your misfortune with the landslide entered the conversation."

Evelyn waves her hand and drawls. "Oh, it weren't nothin' but a thing."

Carter nearly chokes.

"It was jus' a little ol' dab a mud on the grass followed by fireworks and a bonfire. Don't know what all the fussin' was about." With her eyes sparkling mischievously in the candlelight, Evelyn places both elbows on the table, leans forward and blinks.

The eyes above the regal nose open slightly wider than they had at Carter's chicken-fried squirrel comment. "Good Lord," the woman mutters to herself.

Evelyn blinks again. "Thanks for stoppin' an' sayin' hi. We sure does appreciate it."

The aristocratic head pulls back on the aristocratic chicken neck – my bad – the *slightly-more-than-middle-aged neck.* Alexis and Mr. Alexis move on.

Carter is choking back laughter when he leans forward and halfway across the table. "What brought on all that?"

"The way she looked down her nose at you for saying chicken-fried squirrel," Evelyn fumes. "As if *we* answer to *her.* And what was this?" Evelyn angles her head to display her necklace. "I felt like telling her: Las Vegas must have lost their sign because there it is around your saggy old neck."

Carter laughs some more.

"The only reason she complimented me was to get a compliment in return. That garish collar of potpourri bling was genuinely hideous. I half expected to see flashing red LED's wired into it."

"Wow. You are on it tonight."

"Well, she pissed me off. If Cass had been here, she would've kicked her droopy old ass for being such a..." Evelyn glances around, "...you know what."

Carter begins to look under the table and at his sides as if he'd lost something. "You know I came here with this lovely, sophisticated woman and somehow ended up with an alley-cat that's hissin', spittin' and looking for a fight. You haven't seen my date, have you?"

Evelyn laughs. "It could have been worse. If Sausalito had been here, he might have re-killed that thing she had across her shoulders."

Carter subtly imitates Sausalito's snarl, low growl and death-shake with his teeth clenched on an imaginary hide. When Evelyn laughs, a few more heads turn their direction with displeased frowns. Carter laughs. "Oh my God, Evelyn. We are no longer socially acceptable. We have become hillbillies."

The Bentley's bonnet reflects the late-night skyline as it

pulls up to the red canopy where Carter and Evelyn stand arm in arm waiting for their vehicle. Carter steps forward to open the passenger door for Evelyn while the valet gets out and holds the driver's door for Mr. Chatsblythe.

As they drive away, Evelyn touches Carter's leg. "We may have fallen from society's good graces tonight, but at least the Maître'd didn't throw us out."

"I noticed him looking at us with a raised eyebrow a couple times."

"What a bunch of snobs." Evelyn laughs, looks out the window a moment at the glistening city nightlife, then angles her head and redirects her gaze to Carter. "Are you still hungry?"

"I *am*."

"You know, I am too. Cass mentioned a cheeseburger the other day and I haven't been able to think of anything else since."

"Are you serious?"

"Drive thru," Evelyn suggests with a devious glint in her eye. "Let's be naughty, break all the rules, and chow down in Bernard's precious Bentley."

Carter throws his head back and howls ecstatically. *"Oh my God. This is the best date ever."*

"Next date night let's wear flannel and plaid an' go to one a them family-style restaurants an' get us some a that there chicken-fried critter," Evelyn suggests.

Carter laughs loudly. "You got yerself a deal, lady."

The estate's numerous ornate lanterns sparkle in the cool midnight air. The Bentley slows for the iron gates of the Chatsblythe's mansion to open. It then accelerates through and comes to a stop near the front steps. Dim light filters through the drawn drapes and closed shutters of the windows. The Bentley's engine cuts. The doors open.

153

Evelyn exits the car barefoot and laughing. Carter's jacket is draped over his shoulder and his tie is hanging from his finger when they come together in front of the car for a passionate kiss. With hands roaming, they stumble toward the steps where they kiss again and begin to giggle. More giggles, interspersed with midnight shushes accompany their clumsy, intertwined ascent to the door.

With their giggles now completely unabated, the couple spills into the silent house and cavorts about with passionate whispers in the shadows of the dimly-lit entrance. The heels she carries are left on the credenza as they stagger through the foyer. A kiss and wildly groping hands cause them to fall silent at the base of the staircase.

The kiss continues.

It continues some more.

Sausalito and Cincinnati look at each other from the eighth step up on staircase where they sit watching. "Don't you guys gotta breathe sometime?" Cincinnati finally asks.

"Oh dear God!" Evelyn and Carter push away from each other. "What in the hell are you two doing out here?" Evelyn demands as she pulls her clothing back in place.

"It's after one o'clock in the mornin'. We was worried about you so we was waitin'," Cincinnati innocently replies.

Sausalito puckers his lips, shakes his head and stands. "You two is somethin' else." He places his hand on his little brother's shoulder. "Tol' you they was fine. Can we go to bed now?" Then without waiting for an answer, Sausalito nudges Cincinnati up the staircase.

While Sunday morning has dawned, it has not dawned early for the Chatsblythe household. The kitchen is not-that-tastefully (no pun intended) decorated by the fairly substantial mess created by the first risers — who would be the boys who have made their own breakfast burritos.

Both boys are sitting at the table in the nook eating when Carter and Evelyn, wearing robes, enter the kitchen. "Good morning." Carter nods his head as he greets the boys.

"'Mornin'," Sausalito replies, then looks at the current time of 10:23 a.m. with the same disapproving expression the couple had seen on his face at 1:17 a.m.

Ignoring it, Carter looks around at their mess. "I see you've made breakfast."

"Missus Gilbert showed us what to do," the teen answers briefly. "We made two fer you. They's still in the pan stayin' warm if you want 'em."

"Why thank you. That is so considerate of you." Carter anxiously walks to the range while Evelyn holds back and observes the boys with reservation.

Carter removes the lid of the pan, then inspects the contents with pleasant surprise. "Hey, these look good. Hon, would you like one?"

Evelyn closes her eyes and shakes her head more like a shudder than a response. "I'll have fruit." She looks at the boys, then offers a concise, "Good morning."

"Mornin' Missus Chatsblythe," Sausalito replies.

"Oh wow. We are not doing this right," Carter observes. "We are no longer Mister or Missus Chatsblythe. As of a couple days ago, we are a family." He takes a bite of one burrito then drops them both onto a plate. "Hey, not bad, guys. Not bad at all. Oh good, Missus Gilbert made coffee before she left." He retrieves a mug and fills it. He moseys to the table while Evelyn migrates toward the refrigerator. "I know we aren't mom and dad, but could we be Carter and Evelyn instead of Mister and Missus Chatsblythe?"

When Carter plops down at the table, the teen nods. "Okay. We can do that."

"Good." Carter smiles proudly. "By the way, I am really feeling our hike yesterday."

"Me too, a little."

"Wait twenty five years. I'm feeling it a little more than a little."

"What was you doin' last night?" Cincinnati casually inquires of the couple. "There was all kinds a noises coming from yer room."

There is a clatter near the refrigerator, then Evelyn abruptly looks at the ceiling with her lips sucked in.

Carter turns around. "You okay, hon?"

"Fine." She bends to pick up a couple things she'd dropped, then turns toward Cincinnati with flared nostrils. "What did you do, sit outside our door?"

"For a little while."

"*Oh. My. God.*"

"I couldn't sleep."

"Evelyn and I exercise after we've been out," Carter answers seamlessly. "You know, to work off the calories from a large dinner."

"How come you didn't use yer exercise room?" Cincinnati asks as he chomps off another bite of his burrito.

"We actually *have* done that a couple times, but last night we decided it might be better to exercise in our room."

"Oh," the boy says with disinterest and chews his bite of burrito.

Carter chances a quick glance Sausalito's way to find him shaking his head disgustedly. When Carter smiles, Sausalito's nostril raises in disgust.

"So, I have a couple ideas for things we can do today," Carter announces.

"I hope one of them is putting a lock on the *outside* of

156

Mister Nosey's door," Evelyn suggests, still blushing as she joins them at the table with a small bowl of fruit.

"Locks on the outside of children's doors are illegal," Carter advises.

"It shouldn't be." Evelyn's eyes dart over to Cincinnati, then back to Carter.

"So anyway," Carter resumes his thought. "Sundays are typically the day Evelyn and I just like to be home, relax, maybe swim a few laps…"

"Exercise," Sausalito sarcastically adds.

"Occasionally exercise," Carter adds with another devious smile. "But I thought for our first family day, we probably should do something a little more interesting."

"Movie?" Cincinnati asks with a few chunks of food falling from his mouth.

"No. Not a movie. We're not just going to just sit around and stare at something. I want us to do something fun that has some interaction involved."

"We didn't just stare at somethin' when I sawed my movie," Cincinnati interjects. "We talked through the whole movie an' Cass said that's intera-tion. I likes me a movie."

"Yes. I heard that you managed to vacate a whole section of the theater and have it to yourself. Typically films are not a speaking venue. We'll work on that. I thought we could go to the track today."

"The track?" both boys ask.

The Ferrari roars through a wide embanked curve. Moments later, a vintage Aston Martin follows. A smattering of various models of Ferrari, Porsche and Lamborghini also enter the curve. Inside Carter's Ferrari, Sausalito glances between the pavement that has the appearance of being sucked under the car, and Carter, who casually negotiates the track like an old pro. "How fast we goin' now?" he asks.

"One fifteen, but we're still warming up," Carter smiles.

"Lord almighty."

"Can't open it up just yet. Evelyn and I like to play a little tag before we go balls-out." Just then the Aston makes a dash inside the Ferrari's arc on a curve. Carter shouts, "And there she goes!"

Cackling like a witch with both hands firmly at 10 and 2, Evelyn cheers, "Woo-hoo! Kiss my ass, Carter!" While glancing at the Ferrari in the mirror, she laughs some more.

Watching between the cackling witch and the road with wide eyes, Cincinnati grips the armrest on the door with one hand while the other clutches the leather seat. "You people is nuts."

"You should see Cass out here," Evelyn yells over the noise of the car. "She's actually been banned from the track. Carter and I used to bring her as a guest. She should drive Formula One. *That* is a lady that's nuts."

Entering a straight-away, Carter prepares to shift. "Watch this," he says to Sausalito, then clutches, shifts and gives it the gas. With a bone-shaking surge of power, the Ferrari pins their heads to the rests. It launches forward, overtaking the Aston as if it was standing still.

"Holy shit," Sausalito yells. When he forces his head to turn toward Carter, a huge smile has spread across his face because although speed may be a little *Lord almighty* and a bit of *holy shit,* there is nothing quite like a G-force.

The family sits in a booth at the local Black-Eyed Pea. A basket of dinner rolls and cornbread has been decimated. Everyone but Evelyn is devouring a chicken-fried steak with mashed potatoes smothered in gravy. While she quietly eats a salad, the laughter, loud exclamations and proud boasts fire ceaselessly between the guys. "When me and Evelyn had our turn in the Ferrari, we passed you slow-pokes like you was standin' still. In two seconds time the Aston Martin was this big in the mirror." Cincinnati holds his fingers an inch apart.

"He let her by. He was like in second gear," Sausalito argues.

"No. I was giving the Aston all that she had," Carter corrects. "We were doing one twenty nine."

"One twenty nine?" Evelyn questions with a teasing smile. "Is that all you can get out that car?"

"Oh, listen to who's talking shit now." Carter laughs. "What were you doing when you passed us that first time, hon?"

"One forty five." Evelyn smiles demurely.

"Holy shit," Sausalito exclaims and tosses his fork in the air.

Sunday's late afternoon sun is baking the west side of the city when the family emerges from the restaurant. "That was the best food I ever ate." Cincinnati rubs his distended belly. "Even better 'n pizza and I *loves* me a pizza."

"Yeah," Sausalito adds. "Thank you for dinner. It was real good."

"You're both very welcome." Carter flattens his shirt to reveal his distended gut. "I think I might have overdone it a bit myself."

"You're gonna have ta exercise a bunch tonight, huh?" Cincinnati blithely observes.

A smile breaks across Carter's face as he pulls Evelyn into his arm. "You can count on that, buddy boy." When he turns to catch what's sure to be Sausalito's disapproving sneer, the teen has stopped walking and stands rigidly three paces behind them. With narrowed eyes, he looks ahead to where a group of street punks have gathered around the two very expensive automobiles. The punks talk and laugh as they strike poses while leaning on the fenders to take selfies with their phones. When Sausalito starts a low growl, Carter quickly assesses the situation. "Oh shit."

"Now, Sausalito, they're just having fun…" he begins with a very even tone. But Sausalito doesn't stick around to heed or even hear his caution. With narrowed eyes riveted on the teens, Sausalito starts their way with a slow, even stalk, growling all the while. Carter briskly walks ahead of him and presents a wide smile to the punks. "You like those cars?"

A punk/gothic-looking creature with his ears full of rings and multi-colored hair quickly moves away from the fender he'd been lounging on. "Is this your car, man?"

"Yes. Those are our cars."

The creature looks over Carter and the family as they come up to join him.

"You got some sick rides, man," he says as his eyes migrate curiously toward still growling Sausalito.

A tough-looking girl with a tattooed arm and rings in her lips sneers at the family. "You own *both* of these?"

"The Ferrari's mine. The Aston is hers."

"Must be nice," she caustically observes.

"It is." Carter glances toward a more muscular and dangerous-looking type who stands on the far side of the Ferrari. "If you guys want to get a few more photos, that's fine. We'll wait."

The tough, sporting a muscle tee and shredded jeans, steps around the car. "How about a couple photos of me *inside?*"

"Yeah. I don't think so," Carter declines.

Sausalito's growl becomes loud enough that everyone's

head turns his direction.

"What's your problem?" the girl questions. "We ain't good enough to even sit in your cars?"

"It's just not a good idea," Carter explains.

Sausalito's growling gets louder.

"That your dog?" the tough asks. Then without waiting for a response, adds, "You should put him on a leash before something happens to him. Come on, man, quit bein' a dick. We just want a couple pictures."

"I really shouldn't have to explain myself and calling me a dick isn't exactly going to win over my heart," Carter asserts. "I said no and I mean no."

Sausalito nearly barks as he slowly closes in on the teen with very even movements of his long, slender limbs.

"Did he just bark?" The tough laughs. "Seriously. You need to get your boy on a leash 'fore he gets hurt."

Carter positions himself between Sausalito and the tough. "I don't think I *could* get him on a leash. It would probably be a good idea if you all just moved along now."

"You rich asshole," the girl snaps.

When Sausalito turns her way, Carter foolishly extends an arm to hold him back. A lightening-quick gnash of teeth and a threatening lunge causes Carter to yank his arm back and jump out of the way. "Holy crap," he exclaims with the hair on his back standing up. Cincinnati quietly comes forward, then pulls on Carter's shirttail to get him to safety.

"It's best you stay outta the way," he warns. "He's gonna take care a' this an' there ain't nothin' you can do about it. This is his instincts takin' over."

With Carter pulled out of the line-of-fire, the tough throws his arms out and takes a bold step toward Sausalito. "You wanna go, dog-boy?"

With a vicious onslaught of barks, snarls and growls, Sausalito charges. The tough is instantly backed up to the

Aston where without a touch, he finds himself pinned by a very, very wild animal he has no idea what to do with.

The girl thinks she does. She balls a fist, then runs forward to clock Sausalito in the back of the head. His skinny arm shoots out and intercepts her attack. His fingers clamp around her fist, twisting it so that she is instantly forced to her knees.

"You're going to break my wrist," she shouts.

His grip does not relent and his crazed eyes stay on the tough's now slightly terrified eyes. The low growl continues from somewhere deep in his throat.

"Okay, we'll go," the multi-colored creature offers.

"Yeah. We'll just go," the tough backed against the car whispers to the snarling face three inches from his own. "I don't know what you are, but we'll go."

As the girl with the horribly contorted arm whimpers, Sausalito's growl gradually subsides. Then releasing her hand, Sausalito backs up just enough to allow the tough to squeak out from between him and the car. The three punks join ranks, then begin to walk across the lot with their heads turned back and their eyes more on Sausalito than where they are going.

That night, laying in bed together with the lights on, Carter and Evelyn both stare at the ceiling with eyes open wide. "There is something dangerous sleeping in the room down the hall," Evelyn comments.

"I'd have to agree with you on that." Carter nods. "If I close my eyes, I can still see him gnashing at me."

"I can still see the girl kneeling with her arm all twisted around," Evelyn confides.

Chapter Eleven

What Do I Believe?

When the boys walk into the kitchen for breakfast, Carter, Evelyn and Mrs. Gilbert look over at them from their huddle of hushed conversation with uniformly wary expressions.

"Mornin'," Sausalito says with eyes that shift between them. He looks at his brother, then back at the huddle with raised eyebrows. "I s'pose we need to talk."

"Listen…" Carter interrupts.

"I said I reckon we're gonna talk," Sausalito asserts. Without leaving much room for debate, he explains, "I know y'all's worried about what you saw yesterday. It don't make no sense for us to be tip-toein' around it. I got instincts. I ain't like y'all an' I never said I was. I even went out a my way to tell you I weren't."

"He was defendin' the family." Cincinnati joins in his brother's defense.

"An' nippin' at you was just a reaction," the teen explains to Carter. "I jus' seen a hand comin'. My vision gets real narrow when stuff is goin' on. It's jus' instincts. I wouldn't never hurt any y'all. I felt bad all night with ever'one bein' quiet 'round me an' all ever since that all happened."

"It's a concern," Carter concedes.

"I know it is." Sausalito nods. "I'm still the same as I

ever was. You jus' know more who I am now. I tol' you I ran with the pack. I tol' you all that."

"That you did. It's just that right now I'm a little afraid to touch you," Carter admits. "I'm a little afraid a household problem might stir up something in you that we don't know how to deal with. Like I said, it's a concern."

"You sendin' us away?" Sausalito asks.

"No. We're not sending you away. We signed papers. Sausalito, you have some superhuman attributes. You're fast as a rabbit, fierce like I've never seen, tough enough to walk home with barely any blood in you – you're amazing. That's frightening to mere mortals like us. Give us time to process this. Halfway. Meet us halfway while we sort this out."

"Okay. I jus' want it out in the open."

"Okay. I guess we did need to do that. I'm glad you addressed it."

Sausalito glances at the women's still apprehensive expressions.

"Listen," Carter begins anew. "Raymond called last night to ask if you were feeling up to going over to the bank to speak with Missus Conley today. I told him you probably were ready to do that. He said he would arrange a meeting. Evelyn will go with you in case you need anything signed." Carter checks the time. "I have to jet." He kisses Evelyn, then veers around the boys on his way out of the room.

Sausalito sidesteps and places his hand on Carter's shoulder as he passes. Carter stops eye-to-eye with the teen whose voice is as clear as his eyes. "Yesterday was real fun. I did a lot of thinkin' last night. I never had anywhere near that much fun before. Workin' an' learnin' was Mama's biggest concern. I wants to learn me how to drive. I don't think cars is bad. We thank both a' you." Sausalito looks between Carter and Evelyn. "I won't never forget what we done yesterday. It was fun as hell. I'm sorry I ruint it." The corners of the teen's mouth droop and he takes his hand off Carter's shoulder.

While gnawing on his lip, Carter considers the sincere young man before him. "You didn't ruin anything. You were protecting the family." With a half smile, Carter pulls the slender teen into a hug and pats his back. "I never said thank you. That was remiss of me. Thank you for protecting your family." He pushes Sausalito back and holds him at arm's length. "Maybe I'm not afraid to touch you after all. And…" Carter smiles, "I would love to teach you how to drive." After a crooked smile and a brief hug for Cincinnati, Carter steps out of the kitchen.

That afternoon in the exercise room, Sausalito is eeking out a set of bench press on a machine while Cincinnati watches him. "You nervous 'bout goin' to the bank?"

"A little." Sausalito finishes a rep, releases the bar and sits upright. "Are you?"

"I'm jus' 'fraid there'll be cops an' the welfare people there to take up away."

"I don' think it's a trick. Mama had me meet Missus Conley a couple times so we wouldn't be strangers when she passed. It's been a spell since I seen her, but Mama said she's a good woman." Sausalito massages his muscles. "Carter had six times this much on this. He must be awful damn strong."

"But he's a' scared a you."

"It's 'cause I'm wild an' he don't know what to do 'bout wild." Just as Sausalito breaks a crooked smile, growls lowly, then playfully springs off the bench. Cincinnati shrieks, and the chase is on. They are halfway across the room when Evelyn walks in and immediately recoils. Their playful game of chase ends abruptly. Sausalito is quick to hold his hands up innocently. "We was jus' playin'."

After looking at both boys cautiously, Evelyn smiles briefly and uncomfortably. "Bernard has the car ready."

With a sick look and suddenly subdued demeanor, Sausalito takes hold of his little brother and guides him ahead of himself out of the room. "I feel like we's goin' to the ex'cutioner," Cincinnati laments.

The Bentley, with the boys in back and Evelyn riding shotgun with Bernard, pulls into the bank parking lot. It glides silently to where Raymond's Mercedes is parked and stops in an adjacent spot. Raymond's door opens. He stands and smiles generously. The boys step out of the Bentley and force sick half smiles in return.

"Good afternoon, Evelyn," Raymond greets, then walks over to give her a brief hug and a peck on the cheek.

"Good afternoon, Raymond." She kisses him back. "I brought the paper."

"Good. Good," he replies. "You ready boys?"

Both shrug, then take the attorney's hand for an uncertain shake.

"Now, just a reminder," the elderly man cautions, "my biggest concern is that you don't volunteer any information that isn't specifically asked of you. That's especially important with any details about your mother's death. The law tends to take a different view on matters like that. They don't like to see us burying our loved ones in our back yards or burying them without someone declaring them officially dead and determining the cause first." He places a hand on each of the boy's backs, then walks between them toward the entrance of the bank. "Missus Conley seemed like a very nice lady on the phone; very cordial and very well informed," he comments to the complete disinterest of the boys.

The bank lobby is a cavernous affair with a high ceiling and marble walls. Raymond approaches a reception desk where he signs in, then speaks with the receptionist in warm tones. While the boys look around in wonder at the magnificent lobby, a woman comes out of a large office and briskly strides their way. She breaks a smile to see the boys. "Sausalito," she juts out a hand for a shake. "How good to see you again. I don't know if you remember me. I'm Missus Conley."

Sausalito squints his eyes as if to recall her, then nods with a degree of reservation, and shakes her hand.

"You must be Evelyn." Mrs. Conley extends her hand to Evelyn. After Evelyn and she have clasped hands, the banker turns to Cincinnati. "I'm betting you're Cincinnati."

The lad morosely nods his head and offers his limp hand for a tug.

When Raymond joins them, her hand is extended one last time. "Mister Bartel, I presume."

"You presume correctly, Madam."

"Won't you step this way?" With a grand gesture, she directs them toward her office.

The placard on her door identifies Mrs. Conley as the President of the bank.

As they walk in, Cincinnati leans to his brother with a very audible whisper. "Ain't no cops yet."

"Do you think you're in trouble?" the bank president asks as she walks around her desk. Both boys shrug. "I can assure you that you are not. Won't you all have a seat?" As all settle into chairs, she continues in a more subdued tone. "Sausalito, it's been a while since we've seen each other but I see that you are becoming a fine young man. And Cincinnati, I have heard much about you. It's good to finally meet you." She takes a moment to look with compassion at both boys. "I understand your mother has passed away. She was a very dear friend of mine. You have my deepest sympathies."

The boys nod.

"But of course we're all here for business. Before we can speak openly, I need to cover my bases so I'll need to see the guardianship document."

Evelyn pulls it from her purse and passes it across the desk.

The woman inspects it, then lays it down. "I will need a copy of that. We'll just hold it there as we will have other documents to copy as well. Mister Bartel, I've heard only good things about you from the community. May I see your identification? Missus Chatsblythe, I'll need yours as well." After examining their driver's licenses, she adds them to the stack to be copied. "What can I do for you today?"

Raymond prompts Sausalito with a gentle nudge. "Well, uh, Mama said we was to see you when she passed. She said you'd arrange livin' expenses an' all that," Sausalito replies. "Mister and Missus Chatsblythe is takin' real good care of us an' we don't need no money, but Mama said it a lot that we was to talk with you after she passed."

The bank president leans forward on her desk and smiles warmly. "Sausalito, your mother had very different ways from most people. As her health began to fade, she and I spoke many times and at great depth of how she wanted to pass things on to you. There are some things you don't know."

"Is we goin' to a orphanage?" Cincinnati inquires.

"No." Mrs. Conley draws a breath. "I've followed you boys' ordeal on the news. Your mother had great faith that

168

you would end up where you were supposed to end up. When Raymond explained to me that the Chatsblythes are paying him to represent you *against* them if need be, I realized your mother's faith had not been misplaced." The woman focuses on Sausalito. "I'm aware of your hospitalization and I know that Missus Chatsblythe signed these papers to get you care. I'm confident you are where you are supposed to be and that you are with the people your mother prayed you'd be with. She asked me not to intervene. She said the Good Lord would work it out. You will not be going to an orphanage. It seems you have your home."

Sausalito nods solemnly. He turns toward his brother, then nods again.

"Does that put your mind at ease?"

"Yes, Ma'am. That's all we cared about." Sausalito begins to rise.

"Not so quick." Mrs. Conley extends her hand and pats her desk. "We have more to discuss." After an apprehensive glance at Evelyn and Raymond, Sausalito settles back into his chair. "It was your mother's wish that I wait for you to contact me. Now that you have, I want to assure you that the full resources of this institution are at your service."

"You must have been a very dear friend," Raymond observes. "Given your different walks of life, I find the fact that you and Loretta had a friendship to be quite remarkable."

"Our walks of life aren't as different as you might imagine." Mrs. Conley smiles. "We were college roommates."

"You was what?" Sausalito bellows.

"Your mother was a brilliant mathematician. I was interested in finance."

"Mama didn't go to no school. You's lyin'."

"Your mother was a much different woman back in the day. She graduated summa cum laude from Bonfort College. When she married, I was her maid of honor and when I married, she was mine."

"No. You's jus' the lady at the bank." Sausalito's face is red as he protests.

Mrs. Conley turns a photo of two laughing young women with their arms wrapped around each other toward him.

He stares at it.

After clearing his throat, Raymond rejoins the conversation. "Although we appreciate your generous offer, I assure you that the boys will be looked out for."

"Allow me to show you something, Mister Bartel." Mrs. Conley slides a folder across her desk. Raymond curiously takes it.

The boys look at each other while Raymond opens it. As he starts to read, he becomes very still. He flips through a few pages, then looks up to Mrs. Conley and clears his throat. "They lived in a small trailer with no electricity or running water," he explains.

"She had her ways." Mrs. Conley smiles.

"This cannot possibly be her," Raymond argues.

"I assure you we only have one client named Loretta Jones. That is her. LSC Holdings Inc.," she mentions as if Raymond will follow. "Loretta, Sausalito, Cincinnati," she explains and adds another slight smile.

Raymond's eyebrows rise. He faces Evelyn. "If I may be blunt, your boys are worth almost as much as you are. It's all in trust, but I believe I will be billing these two boys for my services instead of Carter."

Carter, Evelyn and Mrs. Gilbert sit at the kitchen table

while pots simmer on the range. Outside the French doors, Sausalito and Cincinnati can be seen sitting atop the knoll at their mother's grave. "Unbelievable," Carter comments. "They own or have sold every bit of land up and down this entire valley. Homesteaded by her great, great, great grandparents in what? Eighteen thirty-four? When Sausalito said this was his home and his land, he was right. Unbelievable."

The roar of an engine comes from somewhere in front of the mansion. When it is followed by a screech of tires, Carter's eyes shift to Evelyn. "Floyd's getting tired of cleaning her rubber off the driveway." They wait, then listen as the front door opens. It is followed by the sound of high heels pounding the floor. Momentarily, Cass flies into the kitchen, places her hands on her hips and snorts like an angry bull.

"I knew I should'a taken those boys home. Damnit! Damnit! Damnit!" she stomps her foot with each curse. "I need a drink. Wait, where are they? I want to wring their puny little necks first."

Evelyn inclines her head toward the doors and the grave beyond. "Neither one has said a word to us since they found out."

Cass stomps over to the doors and leans to peer at the boys. "Well, isn't that just dandy? I'm getting my drink." She promptly storms from the room.

"Carter, I'm exhausted," Evelyn says as though she really is. "This guardian/parent crap is hard work. They're up and down and mad and bored and this happens and then that happens and it's only been two weeks and I'm just wiped out."

"I hear ya, hon. I hear ya."

With her heels once again pounding the floor, Cass reenters the kitchen and wipes her mouth with the back of her hand. "I might have just downed a half-bottle of Scotch. It looked like the expensive stuff so I'll have to pay ya back." She takes a guzzle from the glass she holds in her hand. "When you offered to have the whole works trucked over to my place, I should've said *go ahead*." She finishes off the glass, then kicks off her heels. She looks out the French doors again, then walks over to the table, pulls out a chair, and lands on it with a grunt. "I wonder what the marriage laws are in Bolivia. Just so ya know, the little one's mine when you get ready to marry 'em off."

Carter looks squarely at Cass and raises an eyebrow. "Floyd wants you to stop leaving rubber in the driveway."

"Really? You decide to mention a little scratch in the driveway at a time like this? Insult to injury, Carter. Insult to injury."

Ignoring her completely, Carter rises and asks Mrs. Gilbert, "How long before dinner?"

"About a half-hour."

Carter nods, then heads for the French doors.

The boys sit on crossed legs at the foot of the grave. Still in business attire, Carter ascends the winding steps to the top of the knoll. "I hear you boys got some shocking news today."

While Cincinnati looks up expressionlessly, Sausalito's head remains down. He slowly shakes it.

"You care to talk about it?" Carter asks.

Sausalito looks up with blazing eyes. "Ever'thing was a lie. It was a Goddamn lie. Ever'thing. Of the Devil this. Of the Devil that. We Jones's don't go to no schools she always said. But she went to school. She went to college."

"I see."

"She could'a gone to a hospital. *I* went to a hospital," the teen yells and points at himself. "They could'a fixed

172

her. Wasn't nothin' there of the Devil. She told us how to be and what to be and how to believe and what to believe and nothin' she said was true. *Nothin'*. How could she do this to us?"

"I don't know, Sausalito. Maybe she had a reason that isn't clear to us just yet."

"A lie is a lie."

"Sometimes there's a reason. We're human. We don't do things right. Sometimes when we try to be the most right, we're the most wrong. I don't know."

"I'm plenty mad."

"I can see that."

"I don't know if I can ever forgive her."

"Give it time."

"I don't know what I believe no more."

"Maybe to her, wealth was of the Devil, but she couldn't bring herself to walk away from it or maybe she wanted you two to have it. In any case, the way she lived her daily life was true and congruent with what she said."

After a bit of thought, Sausalito nods.

"Maybe that's as good as it gets. We all hold something back. You know? We show others what they expect to see. We show others what we want them to see. We all hide behind something. Remember?"

Sausalito nods again, then comes to his feet and walks face-to-face with Carter. "But what do I believe, Carter? What do I believe?"

"I guess that's something you need answer yourself." Carter's eyes search the teens while the teen's eyes search his.

Sausalito pulls a crumpled slip of paper from his pocket and hands it to Carter. Carter unfolds it. His eyebrows rise. "That's a sizable check."

"That's from the trust – whatever that is – to cover the

things we lost in the slide and the 'splosion. I been thinkin' all afternoon an' there's things I want." Sausalito digs another crumpled piece of paper from his pocket and hands it to Carter.

As he looks at it, Carter begins to nod. "Well, you apparently have the money." Carter looks from one boy to the other and swallows. "So now you don't think this stuff is of the Devil?" Carter clarifies.

"I tol' you. I don't know what to believe but I look around at what we had and what other's got ain't the same. I don't want to be no ignert hillbilly if'in the rest a the world is goin' on without me." Sausalito glances at his brother, who stands, and clarifies, "Without us."

"Having things doesn't make everything better," Carter cautions.

"You should talk." Sausalito sneers.

Carter shrugs. "No. I should *know*." Carter puts a hand to his heart. "If this is empty, no amount of things will ever fill it. If this is full, no amount of things will ever matter." Carter nods toward the list and lifts it ever so slightly. "Keep that in mind."

With a set of his jaw, Sausalito's eyes shift toward the house where Evelyn, Cass and Mrs. Gilbert stand on the patio outside the French doors. Their hands are held to their foreheads to shield their eyes from the western sun as they look back. Carter and Cincinnati turn to see them as well.

"Just like your mother, we're not perfect either," Carter warns. "We might let you down. We might not be what you want. We might irritate you. We might annoy the crap out of you, but that down there – those people – is what you fill this with." He pats his heart again.

Chapter Twelve

A Year Older, a Lifetime Wiser

There are certain disasters that befall mankind. Evelyn Chatsblythe, mistress of the grand estate on Happy Canyon Drive, is no longer a size four. Family dining, cheeseburgers, chicken-fried critter, and pizza night have contributed to a new wardrobe that teeters around a six these days. Worse, it now includes wraps of fabric, Levi's, and flannel rather than form-fitting, designer apparel.

The slightly aging mistress whose child-like wonder and dignified grace are the envy of all, on this particular sunny afternoon, sits with Mrs. Gilbert on the patio drinking iced tea. The easy conversation and laughter of best friends who couldn't be more different or more alike carries over the stillness of the grounds.

The calm, self assured mother of two active teenage boys spends a lot of time at the track. Not the NASCAR track twenty miles across town that the Ferrari club leases on non-race weekends, but the dirt track for motorcycles the boys have made up top on their land. That's not to say one Sunday a month isn't spent at the NASCAR track anyway. There just ain't nothin' like a Ferrari runnin' balls-out – especially since Sausalito learned to drive it. Turns out the boy has a need for speed.

Out on the vast lawn, Floyd crawls about on his hands and knees next to a pile of freshly dug soil, as he repairs a broken sprinkler head. Mrs. Gilbert looks from his untouched tea sitting in a puddle of condensation to him and back. "Hey Floyd," she bellows. "Let that sit and come drink your tea."

He looks up from his chore, waves acknowledgement, then sets his tools down. He painfully stands and slowly begins to hobble their direction.

Evelyn sips her tea, then leans toward Mrs. Gilbert. "Well, I suppose you know what's coming up in a couple weeks."

"Your birthday has been on my calendar for a while," Mrs. Gilbert replies. "I was waitin' to see what you were cooking up this year."

"Not much, probably just the family and Cass. We're going to try to combine my birthday with a remembrance for Loretta. We're waiting for Sausalito to get back with us on how he wants that to go."

The eyes of both ladies eyes wander toward the knoll where the Eleanor Roosevelt grows alone on the flat dirt top. "I see Cincinnati up there every now and then. Never Sausalito," Mrs. Gilbert shares.

"I know." Evelyn shrugs. With Floyd nearing, Evelyn wipes the sweating glass off with a napkin, pats the bottom dry, then with fingers whose nails are no longer manicured, hands it to the filthy, gnarled hands of the gardener.

Floyd arches backward, straightens, takes a good swallow, then issues a gruff warning. "Them boys break another sprinkler head, they're fixin' it. I told 'em fifty times to keep them damn bikes of theirs on the trail and not cut across the grass. Yesterday I saw their tracks across the lawn and this mornin' we was shootin' a geyser of water straight up in the sky."

"If you need Carter and I to say something to them, let me know. And if they need to fix something, we'll make sure they do it," Evelyn assures.

A grumble from the old man is followed by another guzzle of tea.

The half mile radius of raw, eardrum-shattering combustion that emits from the dual five-inch pipes of Sausalito's truck begins to echo off the canyon walls. This would specify that school has adjourned for the day and that he and Cincinnati are now coming home. A sparkle glistens in Evelyn's very ordinary hazel eyes when she smiles at Floyd. "I'd say those are your culprits now."

"Damn kids," Floyd grouses. "They damn near killed me when they arrived here and they been workin' at it ever since. You see the puddle of oil that contraption of his left in the driveway? I told Bernard I ain't cleanin' it up. Damn kids." The roar of the truck suddenly diminishes as the unseen vehicle apparently waits for the estate's gates to open. The relative silence is followed by a momentary blast of combustion which would indicate the truck's journey is complete. But lest the neighbors breathe a sigh of relief prematurely, the engine revs to about five – window rattling, pampered dog frightening, rich folk annoying – grand before the engine becomes still. "Damn kid," Floyd mumbles. "I told him he don't have to rev the engine like that 'fore he shuts it down. Just turn the damn key and park the leakin' piece of shit over a goddamn pan."

Evelyn and Mrs. Gilbert glance at each other with suppressed smiles. A minute later, *"MOM,"* is shouted from inside the mansion.

Evelyn tilts her head back and yells, *"PATIO,"*

One minute later Cincinnati shows up at the French doors wearing school clothes accessorized with a bright red backpack slung over his left shoulder. His hair is stylishly coiffed around his face that is now morphing into adolescence. He's grown a good three inches and put on twenty pounds since the day of his arrival.

"Oh, *there* you are," he comments as he steps outside.

"I said, patio," Evelyn defends.

"I didn't hear you." Cincinnati shrugs his backpack off onto an adjacent table and raises the handful of cookies he obviously harvested on his trip through the kitchen. He stuffs one of them onto the conveyor that is his mouth. Without assistance from his hand, the cookie is transported into his face while he pulls a cell phone out of his pocket with his other hand. He pushes a couple buttons with his thumb, then while looking at the screen, laughs in spite of having a full mouth. He quickly types something on the screen while he chews, then swallows the cookie. "Can I have a sleep-over?"

"Who are you inviting?" Evelyn asks.

"Jesse, Kyle, Fabio and Skeeter."

"Only four?"

"The other guys are busy," Cincinnati explains, then throws his head back ecstatically. "I *love* having friends!" He places another cookie on the conveyor, reads a message on his phone, laughs, then types something. The phone goes back in his pocket. He swallows. "So?" He looks back at Evelyn.

"When?"

"Tomorrow night." Cincinnati glances over at the gardener who is sipping his tea. The boy nods an uncertain greeting at Floyd's wrinkled evil-eye that leers at him over the glass.

Evelyn tips her hand toward the housekeeper. "It's fine by me but Missus Gilbert's the boss."

"So, can I?" Cincinnati redirects his request to the housekeeper.

Mrs. Gilbert clears her throat. "Do ya think even *one* of ya could actually hit a toilet this time? It looked like you boys had piss fights in your bathroom. I don't mind the extra cookin' or the cleanin' but I ain't moppin' up your piss."

"Okay. We'll be more careful, geesh."

"Better yet, none of your little pals are leavin' until I inspect the bathroom and if it ain't par, you and your friends are cleanin' it."

"Okay. Geesh."

"Don't geesh me again. I don't deserve geesh from you."

"Okay, fine. We'll clean it up. *Sooooo*?"

Mrs. Gilbert smiles. "I love you having friends too." She winks at the boy then flashes a tiny smile.

"Thank you." Cincinnati wraps his arms around the big woman, stuffs another cookie in his mouth, then takes out his phone. He reads, groans, then types. The phone goes back in his pocket. "Can we pick 'em up in the limo? They thought that was super-cool last time."

"You need to ask Bernard," Evelyn advises. "You *do* realize I haven't gotten a hug yet."

Cincinnati walks around the table and bends to hug the woman who has become his mother. "Bernard was yellin' at Sausalito when we pulled in. He's mad as hell about something. His eyes were all bulging out and veins poppin' up all over his forehead. I better ask him tomorrow."

Just then Sausalito storms out of the French doors. "I'm gonna punch your chauffeur in the mouth one of these days. Bitch, bitch, bitch. My truck this and my truck that." Although windblown, Sausalito's hair is also now cut and nicely styled. He wears a letter jacket. The pins affixed to it prove he's a natural for the track team (bein' raised by wolves and all). Still skinny as a rail, he's getting a man look to his face. He bends to briefly put an arm around Evelyn and Mrs. Gilbert, then looks at the gardener whose eyes are squinted hatefully and whose jaw is clenched so that his chin nearly touches his nose. Sausalito nods a wary greeting, then resumes his rant. "Now the old turd wants me to park over a pan…"

"*I* want you to park over a pan," Floyd bristles. "Your damn truck is ruinin' the driveway leakin' oil like it is. Why don't ya fix the damn thing? And I got a bone to pick with you boys riding your motorbikes across the damn grass." He points toward the perimeter of the grounds with his gnarled finger. "You got a path you already tore the heck outta. You break the damn sprinkler heads when you two tear across the lawn and you're gonna start fixin' 'em when you break 'em."

Sausalito stares back at the gardener, flares his nostrils, says nothing, throws his hands up, then heads back into the house.

"Hey! Are we ridin'?" Cincinnati calls out, then chases after his brother.

"Damn kids," Floyd mutters as he heads back to his broken sprinkler head.

Mrs. Gilbert reaches over, pats the top of Evelyn's hand consolingly, smiles warmly, then rises and gathers up the empty glasses.

"Here they come," Carter announces to Mrs. Gilbert from where he stands at the French doors. The distant canyon wall and the scar left from the slide has been mended and blended into the steep terrain by LSC Holdings. New vegetation is taking root beneath straw and biodegradable plastic mesh. Two motorcycles wind down the hillside on a path not much wider than a game-trail. Wearing helmets

180

and full leathers, the boys skillfully maneuver their machines down the incline.

Evelyn, clothed in denim and wearing a helmet, sits on the seat behind Sausalito with her arms wrapped around him and holding on for dear life. The bikes no sooner clear the treacherous descent before the throttles open up. Both bikes lift up on their rear wheels and the engines' roar nearly drown out Evelyn's shrieks. They race along the edge of the grounds behind the gardens, fountain, and pool-house, then chase one another along the estate wall headed for the garages out front. The noise is absolutely searing. "Our neighbors love us," Carter comments.

"Don't be so sure." Mrs. Gilbert raises an eyebrow as she walks to the table with a covered platter in her hands. "Housekeepers talk and the Chatsblythes have been on the Happy Canon shit list ever since the landslide."

"I hear ya. I hear ya."

"Between Sausalito's truck and the bikes, I'd say you're about waist deep in poo. You know how rich white folks like their quiet."

After a few moments, the boys and Evelyn enter the dining room in riding apparel and stocking feet. "I'm fine," Cincinnati protests. Midway up his leg is a bloody gash in his leather pants.

"Could I at least look at it?" Evelyn argues.

"Mom, it's fine. It stopped bleeding a half-hour ago."

"Maybe you ran out of blood a half-hour ago. After dinner I *will* look at it and do not sit down without washing your hands." Evelyn points both boys out of the room. "Bathroom, move it," she orders. When she turns to Carter, her tone sweetens. "Hi hon." Evelyn slides her arms around Carter's middle. "We were riding."

"I noticed. Did Cincinnati have an accident?"

"He was going too fast and shot off the track into a tree."

"I wasn't going too fast," is immediately yelled from a nearby bathroom.

"Okay, you were going too *slow* and shot off the track into a tree," Evelyn yells in the general direction of Cincinnati's yell. She turns back to Carter. "I think part of a branch is still in there."

"You know you don't have to come with us each time," Sausalito says as he reenters the dining room waving his hands to dry. "I can handle an emergency."

"Unless *you're* the emergency," Evelyn disagrees. "Did you actually wash your hands or just get them wet?"

Sausalito rolls his eyes, then wraps an arm around Carter's shoulder. "Hey Carter."

"Hey Sause." Carter returns the arm around the shoulder.

Five preteen boys wearing swim trunks dash out the French doors screaming at the top of their lungs. That means it is Saturday morning at the Chatsblythes. The boys blaze across the lawn toward the pool, tuck into balls, then hit the water like incoming mortars. From then on, screaming, shouting, yelling – really any mode of speech that is conducted at 150 decibels or above is how they will communicate for the rest of the morning. Inside the exercise room, Evelyn is jogging on the treadmill, wearing headphones and keeping an eye on the pool.

A lifted fifteen-year-old Dodge 4X4 extended cab painted in hand-sprayed camouflage is sitting up on ramps in the Chatsblythe's garage. Since Sausalito has discovered music, its radio is on. He and Carter lay on creepers beneath it. "I think this one's coming from the valve cover gasket right there," Carter points to the source of an oil leak.

Sausalito scoots over to see where Carter is pointing. "Okay. A pan gasket and valve-cover gaskets. You think that'll do it?"

"It's a start. The rear seal on the transmission is looking a little shiny, but that will have to go to a shop. I have limits on what I'll get involved in." Both scoot out from under the truck. "You got money?" Carter asks.

The teen pats his rear pocket and gestures a thumbs up.

"Alright then." Carter pulls his keys out of his pocket as he walks toward the Ferrari. When Sausalito falls in at his side and holds his hand out near the keys, Carter pulls them away and stops walking.

"I drive it on the track." Sausalito raises his eyebrows.

"Um, yes, but this is in-town driving with other cars on the road and…"

"On the same roads that I drive everyday to go to school. I've never had an accident. My reflexes are insane, you've said it yourself." The teen continues to hold his hand out and offers at least a partial explanation, "There's something I want to show you."

Carter shakes his head, drops the keys in Sausalito's waiting hand, and mutters, "I don't even let Evelyn drive the Ferrari anywhere but the track."

Sausalito grins as his fingers envelope the right of passage in his hand.

Of course it is a father's secret pride and joy to turn over the reins to his son – or better yet – to be gently coerced into it by a confident young man. So it is with purest pleasure that Carter watches Sausalito readjust the mirrors and seat, start the car and fasten his belt. The Ferrari is skillfully maneuvered out of the garage. The gates open and the car moves down the road at a reasonable rate of speed.

As traffic begins to increase along a boulevard of restaurants and strip-malls, Sausalito negotiates well. Carter's pleasantly-surprised smile continues to be stuck to his face. "So, the thing I want to show you is a little bit of a detour." Sausalito checks the mirrors and changes lanes. He flips the signal again as they near an intersection, then turns into a residential area. Sausalito winds down a few streets lined with pleasant homes sprawled on spacious lawns. He slows, then pulls to a curb.

He points toward the side yard of a home on a corner lot. "See that right there?"

"The gazebo?" Carter asks with absolutely no clue as to why he's being shown a gazebo.

"Yeah. You wanted to know what I wanted up on Mama's grave. I think one of those would be nice. Maybe with some more of those Eleanor Roosevelt roses around it. It'd be real pretty. I showed this to Cincinnati yesterday and he thinks so too."

"Okay." Carter nods. "We'll get that done."

Sausalito chews his lip while his eyes remain on the gazebo. "Could we do it before the remembrance?"

"Yes. We can do that. We weren't sure you wanted to do one."

Sausalito nods, still chewing his lip. "Yeah. I do. You've been real good to us. I want you to know I appreciate it."

"Our pleasure. Our privilege, really."

A Nissan passes by, slows, then comes to a stop. The reverse lights come on. It backs even with the Ferrari where it again stops. A couple teenage girls sit in the front seat. The one at the wheel with flowing blonde hair and sparkling eyes smiles. "Hey Sausalito. I thought that was you."

184

"Hey Brittany."

"Nice car." Brittany's eyes focus beyond Sausalito to examine Carter a moment. "Is that your dad?"

"Yeah. I was just showing him your gazebo."

"Okay." She smiles sweetly. "I'll see you later,"

"Okay."

The Nissan pulls ahead, eventually turning into the driveway of the corner house. The Ferrari's signal begins to flash. It cautiously pulls away from the curb, burns a U on the roadway, and starts back toward the main drag. Carter watches the side of Sausalito's slightly red face. After a couple blocks, Carter simply asks, "Brittany?"

Sausalito turns toward him with a shy but somewhat victorious smile and shrugs.

Chapter Thirteen

Things Lost

Six trellis arches of white lattice form the sides of the new gazebo newly built atop the knoll. A tiered roof of red clay tiles reflect the late-day sun. Five Eleanor Roosevelts, one for each side, are planted beneath the arches. A stone path enters the sixth side, then becomes a circle to form a floor over the unmarked grave. Succulent ground cover cloaks the earth that surrounds the structure. The family, including Mrs. Gilbert, stands inside, admiring not only it, but the framed views of the grounds from its arches.

"See the fountain, that's what Mama would'a liked best," Cincinnati boasts proudly. "I picked this spot just for that reason,"

"You did very well, little brother." Sausalito pats his shoulder.

"You know what I find amazing?" Carter proffers. "It's just such a natural compliment to the grounds. We didn't know anything was missing until this was here. Now I look at it and think, how could it be any other way?"

"It does fit nicely," Evelyn agrees.

"You boys did real good," Mrs. Gilbert adds. "Your mama would be pleased as punch to see what you chose to remember her with. It has life to it. I was afraid you'd come up with some gaud-awful stone monstrosity. For a country girl, there could be nothin' finer than this."

Sausalito smiles crookedly as he nods thoughtfully.

"And we got it done just in time." Carter smiles. "I hear us guys are in charge of the decorations for the big birthday tomorrow." He winks at Evelyn.

Both boys smile mischievously. "Little brother's got some ideas…" Sausalito warns.

Cincinnati's smile stretches across his face.

"Oh geez." Carter puts a hand to his forehead.

Cincinnati grabs Carter's hand and begins to pull him from the gazebo. "Come on, I'll show you what I'm thinkin'." After taking a couple steps down the rock path, Cincinnati turns to Evelyn and Mrs. Gilbert. "You two stay here while we show him. No snooping. Stay here until we say you can come down." He then hustles Carter down the steps. Sausalito holds out his hands and shrugs helplessly at the women, then follows.

As the guys wind down the stairs, both women look at one another and laugh. "You realize he's at that age where he's likely to think a little off-color…" the housekeeper cautions.

Evelyn takes the housekeeper's large, course hand with her slender, smooth hand. Their fingers intertwine. "You know, it's going to be just us and Cass tomorrow so, however embarrassing, I'm actually looking forward to the surprise." Still holding Mrs. Gilbert's hand, Evelyn looks around the gazebo. "This is beautiful, but what she left us is more beautiful."

"You know, you did something beautiful too."

"I did almost nothing. I can't tell you how much I've come to love those boys."

"Oh lady, you tell me every time you get on the back of that motorcycle to go up the hill. Every time there's five little heathens splashing in the pool and your eyes don't leave 'em for a second, you tell me. Hell, every time you eat greasy ol' pizza with 'em, you tell me. Every time you laugh, you tell me. I know how much you love those boys."

"I never could hide anything from you."

"You wasn't tryin', but no, you never could."

They look down and watch the boys as they lead Carter around the pool. Cincinnati's laughter carries on the breeze. "Don't say I didn't warn you." Mrs. Gilbert laughs, then pats Evelyn's hand as she releases it. "I got supper to get on the table so I'm headin' down whether Mister Bossy likes it or not." Evelyn watches the solid housekeeper walk along the path, then start down the steps. She looks around the gazebo, then thoughtfully steps forward, looks up inside its roof, and puts her finger to her mouth.

Cincinnati is not the only one planning a surprise. The women have joined forces to create a little surprise of their own; so on the morning of the remembrance, the men have been banished from the mansion and grounds. Therefore three dirt bikes are ripping up the hillside behind the mansion at first light. As Carter and the boys crest the ridge, the noise muffles, fades, then disappears. The enclave of wealth and privilege returns to the silence of Saturday morning.

For a moment.

The subtle growl of Cass's Carrera on the prowl throbs off the canyon walls as she winds along Happy Canyon Drive toward the mansion. The engine's pulse wanes for the slowly opening gate, then surges into the drive. A moment later the Porsche comes to a mannerly stop under the watchful (if not somewhat evil) eye of Floyd who stands up from the nearby garden he's weeding in the morning cool. Cass's door opens. Their eyes lock. The beauty stands, adjusts her outfit of jeans, flannel shirt, and work boots, then nods at Floyd.

Floyd nods back.

Cass reaches back into the car and picks up a well-worn leather tool belt and slings it over her shoulder. She closes the door.

Cass nods again at Floyd.

Floyd nods again at Cass.

Cass walks up the steps toward the front door of the mansion. Floyd watches her the entire way. She watches Floyd the entire way. Finally, she lets herself in.

"Honey, I'm home," she yells as soon as she shuts the door behind her.

"In the kitchen," Evelyn yells back.

Evelyn, wearing jeans and a sloppy tee shirt, is ransacking a drawer when Cass enters. "Whatcha doin', sunshine?" Cass shifts the tool belt on her shoulder.

"I'm looking for my hammer. I just had it out for... Oh. I know where I left it." With that Evelyn turns to walk out of the kitchen.

Cass follows her through the dining room and foyer, then up the staircase. "I swear, Evelyn. Either you're getting faster or I'm getting slower. Could you drop down a gear?"

"Lots to do," Evelyn calls over her shoulder and waves her hand. "You need to come up anyway. I want to show you my latest project."

"Are you getting a new personality?" Cass asks hopefully.

"Very funny. The old one is just fine, thank you not at all," Evelyn sasses. She sails five paces ahead of Cass as she leads her across the balcony that overlooks the magnificent living room below.

"I preferred it when you were a slug until noon," Cass comments – just the slightest bit out of breath.

"Places to go. Things to do." Evelyn laughs, then

enters the hallway that leads to the master suite. The successive portraits of perfectly photographed classic cheekbones, dignified grace and childlike wonder from birthdays 30 through 42 sit on the floor. In their place hang a hundred mismatched frames that contain a mishmash of poorly centered, slightly out of focus, candid snapshots. Evelyn waves her arm from one end of the interior design catastrophe to the other. "Ta da!"

"Oh sweetie," Cass laments, "what have you done?"

"Check it out." Evelyn beams as she stands back and beckons Cass to come closer.

Cincinnati's gregarious smile and numerous crazy selfies of him and Evelyn seem to dominate the collection. Their unrestrained spirit of joy is balanced by Sausalito's annoyed scowl – usually caught as he's turning away or shielding his face from the pest of Happy Canyon: Evelyn *paparazzi* Chatsblythe. "Oh my. Would you look at those beautiful boys," Cass exclaims as she goes from one to the other. "So gorgeous. So handsome. So available." She turns to Evelyn and speaks as a thoroughly evil villain might speak. "I'm still planning on kidnapping the little one and absconding with him to Bolivia."

Evelyn laughs and smacks Cass on the arm.

"And Carter..." Cass purrs lustfully at several masculine images of him getting out of the pool.

"Would you stop? That's *my* man you're drooling over." Evelyn bops Cass again and both laugh.

"But Evelyn, sweetie, *plastic frames*. I see *plastic frames*. Did you sneak into the dollar store again? There are twelve steps groups for that – *I think* – or at least there should be. Are you going for trailer park casual?" Then Cass falls silent as she leans to look more closely. Mixed among Carter and the boys are just as many photos of Mrs. Gilbert: smiling, laughing, yelling, gathering up plates, standing at the range, over the sink, in her nightgown with curlers in her hair, in her church clothes, neck and neck in an embrace with Evelyn, both of them caught with a sudden turn of their head, wide eyes, and open mouths while gorging on ice cream sundaes in the pantry.

Then there are the photos of grumpy old Floyd: looking up from the garden he's immersed in, riding the mower, yelling at the boys, toothless and laughing behind a birthday cake that is fully ablaze with Evelyn making bunny ears over his head.

Then of Bernard. Cincinnati is his apparent partner in crime because he is with him in every photo: polishing the cars, sneaking off for joy rides, speeding down the canyon road with their arms out the windows, eating hamburgers and fries in the Bentley – and laughing, mostly laughing.

"Evelyn, sweetie," Cass waves her hands at the photographs, "no one takes photos of the staff – much less hangs them with their family."

"Well, they should."

Cass tilts her head to the side.

"I kind of realized that the people who have irritated and challenged me the most in life are also the people that have made me look at myself and helped me the most in life – so why would I not want to love them?"

"Oh, honey, that is so beautiful." Cass looks back at the wall of spontaneous photos, then down at the portraits of posed wonderment that sit on the floor.

Evelyn looks down at them and smiles ruefully. "The thing about getting lost is that you don't know when you've taken a wrong turn. One day you just realize that you aren't where you intended to go. And you aren't who you ever intended to be."

Cass looks at Evelyn solemnly. "Oh sweetie, that is so beautiful."

Evelyn shrugs.

Cass smiles gloriously.

"Oh, there it is!" Evelyn bends, then stands aright holding aloft the tiniest hammer known to man as if it was the Olympic torch.

Cass sneers. "What is that?"

"My hammer."

"Oh dear God." Cass swings her tool belt around and pulls out a rather substantial hammer. "Sweetie, *this* is a hammer. This American made twenty-four-ounce wrecking ball with a carbon-fiber handle and a neoprene rubber grip is the hammer Thor *wishes* he had. You will never build a tree-house in Bolivia with your tiny Malibu Stacy hammer there."

"Good thing that was not my intent," Evelyn sasses, then holds up a small plastic baggie with her other hand that has several dozen small nails and tacks in it. "I'm so thrilled. I love doing construction."

As Cass and Evelyn reenter the kitchen, Cass is asking, "I take it the men-folk have been sent off to slay the wilderness."

"Packed 'em up with breakfast and kicked 'em out the door just before you got here," Mrs. Gilbert confirms as she intercepts the conversation. "We got a good couple hours to get this project done." Mrs. Gilbert looks from Cass's tool belt to the tiny hammer in Evelyn's hand. "Is that all you two brought?" Mrs. Gilbert asks arrogantly, then lifts a cordless drill and power stapler into view. "Floyd hooked me up with power tools." The women respond with the degree of awe appropriate for the moment. They laugh as they cross the room where several plastic totes are stacked near the French doors. Mrs. Gilbert and Evelyn each grab a tote on their way outside while Cass hefts up a step ladder and tucks it under her arm.

"This is going to be so much fun," Evelyn comments as they cross the patio.

"Have I told you lately how proud I am of you?" Cass asks.

"All the time," Evelyn answers. "You tell me all the time."

Three motorcycles banished at first light creep through a densely wooded ridge that runs along a ravine. Branches are either held aside or ducked under while rocks are navigated with feet that keep balance against them. They eventually enter an open area paved by a flat expanse of rock. The lead bike stops and the others pull up behind it.

"You think we're close?" Sausalito calls back to the others.

Carter is the first to cut his engine. "We're close," he responds, then removes his helmet. "And I could use a break." While Carter dismounts, the boys turn off their engines and also pull off their helmets. Carter begins to stretch in the warming rays of the rising sun.

"When I told you I wanted to check this area out," Carter says arching his back, "I didn't know we should have brought machetes or a chainsaw."

"Machetes *and* a chainsaw," Sausalito corrects, then strips off his leathers. "I gotta take a leak."

"Me too." Cincinnati worms out of his gear. "Can we eat now?"

"You bet," Carter assures him.

While the boys stand at each other's sides taking a piss, Carter unpacks foil-wrapped burritos and cups onto the mostly level surface of a rock. He's pouring coffee out of a Thermos when the boys return. "You boys wash your hands?" he asks. They all laugh because washed hands are the antithesis of guy activities. He peels off his jacket and wads it up. They all grab burritos and coffee, then disperse to find places among the rocks where they can each sit and eat.

After a while, Sausalito asks, "You think we're still on our land?"

"Hard to say," Carter replies. "We need to find that spring to know for sure. You know if we can't find it or it's dried up, we can get a surveyor up here and have him figure it out. I assume we've got to be close though." He stands to look over the ravine while he finishes off his second burrito. "According to the map, it empties into this ravine. We could hike around; see if we can find it. We have to blow another hour before they let us come back so we have plenty of time."

Sausalito rises from his place in the rocks and joins Carter. "What are they doing? Why'd they make us leave, anyway?"

"Don't know. They're up to something and worse – I think Evelyn's behind it."

"Yeah, she's been bein' sneaky," Cincinnati agrees as he pops up, crams the remainder of his burrito into his face and wipes his hands on his pants.

"I noticed a little ways back there was an area that was more vegetated and a little greener than other places. Could be the spring we're looking for. You wanna check it out?" Sausalito asks.

"Yeah!" Cincinnati yells, "Let's go!" He takes off down the side of the ravine. "Last one down is a rotten egg."

"Watch for snakes," Carter calls after him and then he and Sausalito begin their much more cautious descent.

194

"Leave it be," Carter shouts as Cincinnati pokes a stick at a coiled rattler that is already agitated and more than ready to strike at anything within range.

"Yeah, leave it be," Sausalito concurs. "You're just makin' it mad."

"I got my knife. Why can't we kill it?" Cincinnati protests.

"It serves a purpose, this is its home, and we aren't going to kill it," Carter insists. "Put down the stick and leave it alone."

"You guys are no fun." Cincinnati flings the stick aside. They allow the rattling snake a wide berth as they pass by. A short distance away, a small spring dribbles a trickle of water into a miniature sandy pool all but concealed by the lush vegetation around it.

Carter warns as they creep closer, "Every animal in five miles knows where this is. Keep your eyes open."

Sausalito looks back at Carter drolly.

"Oh." Carter blushes. "City boy telling a country boy, huh? My bad."

Sausalito clears his throat. "You know, I was thinkin' that our homesteading ancestors prob'ly used this spring for water. They wouldn't have built in a dry creek bed so I wanna look up there," he points at the top of the ravine above them, "and see if I can find any old stuff."

"Good idea," Carter agrees.

"Last one up is a rotten egg," Cincinnati shouts, then tears up the craggy side of the ravine.

"Watch for snakes," Carter yells from behind.

The rusted remains of an old steel drum and a galvanized tub sure enough sit thirty feet above the spring along with the head of spade whose handle has rotted away. "I bet they rigged a pulley and a rope," Sausalito comments as he pokes amidst the brush in hopes of finding more artifacts. While Carter pokes around with him, Cincinnati wanders off by himself.

"Hey guys," the boy calls from not too far away. "Come check this out."

Abandoning their treasure hunt, Carter and Sausalito wander the direction of Cincinnati's voice. Within moments, a white utilitarian building comes into their view. Sausalito gapes to see it. "Carter. That's it. That's the white building I remember."

A dozen things hit Sausalito at once when they step into the clearing. An old block foundation about the size of their former pink trailer sits overgrown with weeds and shrubs. An old Cadillac with a rotted vinyl top and most of its body converted to rust sits under layers of dirt and miles of vines. Every known electrical household convenience sits in a rusted heap near the car. Electrical wires that run from the white building lay cut near the overgrown trailer foundation. A row of power poles without wires line a rutted road now nearly blended with the vegetation along it. Sausalito turns in silence as he takes it all in.

After a moment, he speaks reverently. "I remember this. I remember all this. One day our home was different and then I forgot about this – mostly. This had been our home. Cincinnati, this is where you and I were born." He looks at the car and the various appliances lying in the heap. "This is when Mama changed."

He points at the white building. "I bet you there's a workbench in there that runs down along that wall and under the window."

Carter walks to the door, then peeks in. When he turns back, he nods.

"Oh, wow." Sausalito goes into himself. "I wasn't makin' it up."

Chapter Fourteen

The Remembrance

Carter and Cincinnati's bikes wind down the hillside behind the mansion, cautiously making their way home. When they reach the grounds, they putter, rather than race down the well-worn path that runs along the estate wall. Evelyn and Cass watch them from a table near the pool where they sip margaritas and tan in the mid morning sun. Cass raises her hand to lower her overly-large, bejeweled sunglasses from beneath the brim of her overly-large straw hat. The bikes disappear around the side of the house. She looks back up the hill. "I don't see Sausalito. Hope he didn't go running with the pack again."

"Hmmm," Evelyn ponders. "Something's up." She scoots her margarita over to Cass. "You can finish this off." She stands, grabs a robe off the back of her chair and slips into it. "Cincinnati and I have to go pick up those cakes before the bakery closes at two. I'll find out what's going on." She walks over to Cass and bends around her hat to kiss her on the cheek. "Thanks for your help this morning. I think we did good."

"We did. It was a beautiful idea Evelyn – in more ways than one."

"I hope the boys like it. Enjoy your morning. Don't use up all the sun." Evelyn pats her friend's shoulder and heads toward the house.

Elaborate mock-ups of cakes adorn various shelves and tables in the showroom of an exclusive bakery. Cincinnati and Evelyn walk among them as she leads the way to a counter. Behind a glass display case, men and women wearing paper hats and white aprons frost cakes that look more like sculpture than dessert. Elegantly dressed cashiers wait on a few people at a counter. At Evelyn's approach, a saleslady looks up from the order book she's writing in. "Missus Chatsblythe, good afternoon."

"Good afternoon."

"Two cakes for pick-up as I recall, let me get those for you." She strides away.

Cincinnati leans close and tugs on Evelyn's simple straight dress. "Are all these cakes real?"

"I believe the displays are cardboard, but the frosting is real and don't even think about it. A: it's hard as a rock, and B: I will strangle you if you mess one up."

"You will not strangle me."

"Oh yes I will young man. Right here, right now." Evelyn smiles lovingly, winks, and swipes aside a wayward lock of hair from Cincinnati's forehead. Then she looks up and returns the curious gaze of a man who stands a couple tables over lamely holding a page from an open notebook of cake designs. Evelyn's head pulls back ever-so-slightly. *"Kenneth?"*

The party planner's head angles questioningly and his brow creases. *"Missus Chatsblythe?"*

Evelyn smiles awkwardly. "Imagine running into you here."

"Not so hard to imagine, really." He smiles politely in return. "I think half my life is spent here."

"It's that time again." Evelyn's sweet smile is followed by a slight grimace.

"Oh yes, *the birthday.*"

Cincinnati looks between the two.

Evelyn grins, then proudly positions Cincinnati in front of her. "You probably don't recognize this guy without a rifle in his hands and the barrel pointing at your heart. This is Cincinnati."

Kenneth's eyes grow a bit wide. "Oh. Yes. I do recall the episode – quite vividly in fact."

"I thought you might." The saleslady returns with two small round cakes in boxes. The frosting on the first one says *Evelyn*. The other says *Loretta*. A small cluster of butter cream roses adorns the edge on each. "Oh, these are beautiful," Evelyn gushes. "Just perfect. Exactly as I hoped they'd be."

"I'm so glad you're pleased. It looks like they're all paid for. Is there anything else I can help you with today?"

"No. This is wonderful, thank you." Evelyn hands one cake to Cincinnati, then takes the other. As they turn away, Kenneth continues to watch her and the boy. "Well, nice to see you." Evelyn smiles another small smile.

"Same here."

After taking a couple steps, Evelyn turns back to Kenneth. "I thought of calling you a few times to apologize but I never did. I'm sorry for the way I treated you and that I had made planning my party such an ugly experience for you."

"I also was rude." Kenneth looks again at the civilized boy wearing a cartoon tee shirt and shorts waiting patiently at her side. "I see it worked out okay."

"It did." Evelyn smiles demurely.

Cass stands near a naked statue of a woman at the side of the pool with a balloon in her hand. Cincinnati holds up a piece of tape at her side. "I will not do that," she protests.

"You have to. I'm in charge of decorations." He

laughs loudly at Cass's exaggerated and comical expression of pained discomfort.

"I cannot believe I am doing this." With an abrupt swipe of her hand, Cass takes the tape from the miniature evil mastermind, applies it to the balloon, then sticks the balloon onto the statue's round breast.

Already rolling with laughter, Cincinnati pulls another piece of tape and hands her another balloon. She breaks a snicker while taping it to the other breast. "Evelyn is going to have a cow." Cass looks around at the other statues adorned with party streamers, masks, party hats and sunbonnets. One wears a robe. "What exactly is your theme?" Cass asks as they move on to a male statue.

"I don't know. It's just funny."

They both look at the protrusion on the male statue. "I'm going to let you do that one." Cass steps back.

Then laughing hysterically, Cincinnati tapes a balloon onto the protrusion.

Carter and Evelyn stroll hand-in-hand along Happy Canyon Drive. She wears the same simple frock she'd worn to pick up the cakes and he is dressed in his at-home standard of sandals, shorts and a bold print shirt. He raises his wrist to check the time. "Okay, according to Cincinnati, I think we're allowed to head back now."

The couple changes direction and continues to walk in silence. At a point, Carter shifts his eyes to observe Evelyn's content straightforward gaze. When she eventually notices him watching her, she smiles and leans into him. Their clasped hands part. He raises his arm, wraps it around her shoulders, leans into her and whispers. "Happy birthday, my love."

Evelyn wraps her arm around his waist. "Thank you. This is the best one, ever."

200

"We haven't even had the party yet."

"Doesn't matter. It's already perfect."

"Perfect? Even with Cincinnati in charge of the decorating and Sausalito refusing to come off the hill and Cass as your one and only guest?"

"Perfect," Evelyn confirms. "It's all perfect."

The distant gurgle of a motorcycle causes them to lift their eyes to the canyon wall where they catch a tiny glimpse of Sausalito making his way down the incline behind the mansion.

"See?" Evelyn squeezes Carter tight. "Sausalito's back just in time. Perfect."

Draperies across the expanse of French doors are pulled closed when Carter and Evelyn enter the kitchen. Mrs. Gilbert looks up from the pizza she's preparing. "He's waitin' for ya. I don't know what he's cooked up, but he's been out there gigglin' the whole time." Without a pause or a warning, she bellows, "Hey Cincinnati, they're back."

A moment later, the draperies bulge, then a lump makes its way behind the fabric to an opening in the panels. Cincinnati pops out grinning. "You ready?"

"Ready as I'll ever be." Evelyn grins back.

"Okay, you gotta close your eyes." Cincinnati latches onto Evelyn's hand and pulls her along. "And no peeking."

Sausalito's motorcycle is leaned on its kickstand beside the estate wall. His helmet rests on the handlebars and his leathers are laid across the seat. He stands beside it with shoulders slumped, his head hanging and his hair matted to his scalp. Cass stands with him and speaks consolingly. "I can only imagine how difficult all this is for you."

He shrugs lethargically. "Guess she had her ways."

"We all have our ways, not all of them functional.

201

Whatever her tragedy was, she remained raised two wonderful young men."

Sausalito shrugs.

"However she went about it, she prepared you to be your own person. Even if you don't realize it yet, someday you will understand her wisdom. However imperfectly your mother handled her tragedy, she did the best she could."

Cincinnati's distant laughter interrupts their conversation as it begins to carry across the lawn. Cass and Sausalito turn to see him leading Evelyn from the house toward the decorating calamity at the pool.

Cass places her hand on Sausalito's slumped shoulder and gently jostles him. "Come on, buddy. Let's go remember your mother for who she was and celebrate Evelyn for who she's become."

Sausalito sniffs his armpit. "I stink."

"You know, you look like you stink, so I'll take your word for it. No one's gonna care." Cass reaches up and runs her fingers through Sausalito's hair to fluff and arrange it as best she can. She then takes his hand, clasps it in hers and they begin to walk across the lawn toward the pool.

They are almost there when Evelyn's shriek pierces the air and Cincinnati gales with laughter. A second shriek follows almost immediately. Evelyn then laughs and laughs as she goes from one statue to the next. "Only you would think of this. This is great. This is awesome. Oh, look at that!" She goes on and on. Even Sausalito has begun to smile as he approaches the comical statues and becomes infected by Evelyn and his brother's laughter.

Finally, Evelyn places her hands on Cincinnati's shoulders. "Thank you so much. I will never forget the gift of laughter that you just gave me. It was priceless." She hugs him tightly and then kisses him. When she raises her eyes to Sausalito, he offers a dispirited wave. Evelyn lets her hands fall off Cincinnati's shoulders, walks over to Sausalito and looks deeply into his eyes. "Are you all right?"

"I'm okay. I just needed some time."

"Don't we all," Evelyn agrees as her eyes search his. "Are you ready to go remember your mother?"

He shrugs.

"It's only right that we do that before we do anything for me."

He shrugs again.

Cass turns the teen's hand over to Evelyn, pats it, and steps back. She watches the family walk across the lawn toward the knoll and climb the winding stone steps.

The four of them stop in front of the arched entrance of the gazebo where four lavender balloons are tied to a rail. Cincinnati's forehead wrinkles. "We had to go up the hill for the whole morning so you could tie four balloons to a railing? That was your big construction project?"

Evelyn smiles sweetly and caresses his cheek with her hand. "Take your balloon and come inside."

As Evelyn unties her orb, Cincinnati continues to complain. "Me and Cass did *way* more than this in like a half hour." He takes his balloon with a roll of his eyes and a shake of his head. Carter and Sausalito take theirs with equal puzzlement, then walk inside the gazebo. The original Eleanor Roosevelt rosebush stands alone as if it was a tombstone.

"So, here's my idea," Evelyn begins. "I thought what we would do is say something to the balloon like we're talking to Loretta, then lean outside and let those thoughts fly up to her in heaven." The boys look at her doubtfully. "It's symbolic. It can be something beautiful if you give it a chance. You'll see." She turns to Carter. "Would you like to start?"

"Uh. Okay." He thinks a moment, then after looking a little awkwardly at the boys, focuses on the balloon. "You know Loretta, I obviously never met you, but I feel like I've come to know you at least a little. I guess I'd have to say that I suspect you had a great loss in your life. Whatever happened obviously brought you a lot of pain. I guess what I'd like to say is that once we breathe our last, everything about us is written in stone. You turned out to be kind of an enigma, so now your sons are playing archeologist to piece you together. It's difficult. But I understand pain and I understand fear and I understand that you were only human." Carter thinks a moment, then extends the balloon outside the gazebo. "And it's okay to be human." He lets the balloon fly.

Everyone watches the breeze take it away. It soars into the blue and disappears.

"I'll go next." Evelyn holds the balloon before her as if she was speaking to an old friend. "I guess what I'd like to say is, thank you. Thank you for raising two fine young men. Whatever you didn't do or couldn't do, you poured everything you had into these boys. I somehow feel that you have entrusted them to me and I am so, so grateful for having them here. My gratitude, Loretta, you have my eternal gratitude." Evelyn leans outside the trellis to release her balloon. They watch until it is no more.

All eyes go to Sausalito. He swallows hard, then holds the balloon before him and speaks gruffly. "I'm mad Mama. You raised me and Cincinnati to speak like we were ignorant and live like we were poor when we were neither. You didn't tell me things I needed to know. In that picture of you and Missus Conley, you were laughing and I don't ever remember you laughing like that. I wanted to see you laugh. I know this is supposed to be all sweet and loving,

204

but Mama, I'm mad and I've been mad and I'm gonna be mad.

"You died on the floor of a crappy old trailer when maybe you didn't even have to die at all. The things you said were bad, weren't bad, Mama. Everyone's trying to tell me to see you differently, but this is how I feel." He looks at his little brother and shrugs weakly. He holds his balloon outside as if to release it, but then pulls it back inside, kisses it, then releases the balloon.

When Sausalito turns to look Cincinnati, the boy's head is bent backward, his eyes focused above, and his lips are parted. Hung inside the ceiling of the gazebo is the embroidered silk scene of heaven taken from Evelyn's retreat.

Angels look down with benevolent eyes and hands reached out to help. Some look up, astonished, with arms spread wide in glory. Angels in flowing robes of satin with wings of whitest down are in flight. Cherubim frolic. Others play harps. Eyes painted on porcelain look impassively at human eyes that look up at them in wonder.

"Hon," Carter speaks reverently. "This is beautiful."

Cincinnati turns from angel to angel as if to connect with each of them.

"I never looked up," Sausalito either admits or explains.

"We rarely do," Evelyn agrees. "We rarely do."

"But these angels are *your* angels," Cincinnati says when he finally looks at Evelyn.

"It was time to pass them on." She smiles. "All my angels are now living." She cups her hand to the contours of Cincinnati's cheek. "Now it's your turn to say something to your mother."

Cincinnati looks at his balloon. He looks at the angels. He looks at the view of the fountain. He looks between them all again, then walks outside the gazebo and selects a rosebush between the fountain and the angels. "I'm not gonna send it yet. I want Mama to be with us today." He kneels and ties the balloon's ribbon to the bush. It tugs against the small branch, straining to leave even as Cincinnati rises. "Mama, I know you're here and I want you to see how it all worked out." He goes to Evelyn and wraps his arms around her. She returns the hug and leans over to kiss the top of his head.

Carter opens his arms to guide the family out of the gazebo and down the steps. Cass has waited for them on the lawn with camera in hand. "Let me get a picture. How about over there on the fountain?" She waves them over to the splashing water. "Let me get a picture of everyone on the fountain."

While Evelyn sits on the rim and crosses her legs, Carter kicks off his sandals, steps into the churning water, comes up behind Evelyn and wraps his arms around her. They laugh as he bends and nuzzles her neck. Cincinnati climbs up on the rim, lays over Evelyn's lap, then props himself on his elbow and faces Cass. As Sausalito takes his place at Evelyn's side, she and Cincinnati begin to cuddle playfully and laugh.

"Okay, now everyone quit squirming," Cass directs as she kneels to get a better perspective. "Look this way."

But Sausalito doesn't turn or smile. He continues to observe Evelyn. "That was real nice, what you did for our mama."

Evelyn smiles demurely, reaches up, lovingly cups her hand to his cheek, then turns to face the camera. The sparkle in her perfectly ordinary hazel eyes is framed by fine wrinkles that fan out across her temples.

Sausalito's eyes never leave the woman who has become his mother.

206

"Okay everybody, look at me and say cheese," Cass instructs.

No one does.

Cincinnati twists around to look up at Evelyn.

Evelyn's head falls back in laughter.

Carter looks down lovingly at his wife.

Sausalito leans down to kiss Evelyn on the cheek.

Lorretta's balloon comes loose from the rosebush and soars heavenward against a deep blue summer sky.

The shutter snaps.

Perfect.

Thank you for reading.

I hope you enjoyed the story.

Please visit
RogerLGreene.com